LONDON ROCKS

Brenda Lee Browne

HANSIB

First published in Great Britain by Hansib Publications in 2018

Hansib Publications Limited
P.O. Box 226, Hertford, SG14 3WY

info@hansibpublications.com
www.hansibpublications.com

ISBN 978-1-910553-72-5

A CIP catalogue record for this book
is available from the British Library

Design & Production by Hansib Publications Ltd
Printed in Great Britain

This book is dedicated to the original sound men, especially The Lads, Eric G. Antonio and Kendra Lion; my son, Jordan, who designed the cover, an artist who inspires me everyday; my writing family and a special thank you to Arif Ali for gifting me this publication; and to Joanne C. Hillhouse who believed in Dante from day one. And thank you Leonard Tim Hector for the pen and the push.

BLUES DANCE

At first glance, the dark room appears empty, until a shaft of light illuminates a sea of heads, side by side and face to face, locked for a moment in a haze of sweet, yet pungent smoke.

The air is charged with sexual, youthful possibilities as bodies move slowly in time to the music.

As the door closes, another song begins. Bodies mould into one form, hips dipping, knees slightly bent, and hands tighten around waists.

Dante pulls the petite brown skin girl closer. Her hair smells of Dax, the same hair pomade he uses. She moves with him; he leads, she follows. He slows his movements until his penis strains against his Italian Farah slacks – she does not pull away. He has to count backwards to stop himself from exploding against her.

Sweat beads form on Dante's brow and sweat trickles down his spine. She has 'it', the thing he and his boys joke about: the feeling that this woman is made just for you.

The music changes tempo; Dante holds on steadying his thoughts. He wants to kiss her but she is no easy girl, the kind you can kiss anywhere and treat anyhow, a sign of no upbringing. No, he feels he needs to respect this brown skin, especially if he wants to see her again.

He whispers, "Hi," into her ear. She wriggles against him and purrs, "Hi," as he rests his chin on the top of her soft, Dax infused hair. She feels real good, and he thinks of his ex, Sheila, the mother of his little girl, who often dances as though she is angry with him.

Dante and Sheila met when they were both thirteen, second period, maths. Dante was sitting in his usual seat at the back, his chair twisted side on as he focused all his energies on doodling musical notes on his maths' book cover.

The door opened and a girl entered. Her ponytail seemed to have been placed on her head by some sort of magnet, for every strand of hair was perfectly in place. Her oval face was blemish free, but it was her eyes that caught his attention – they were green, cat's eyes that hinted at a secret.

Dante was hooked. They started going out, and by sixteen, they were having regular sex. She went and got the pill. At seventeen, she wanted them to move in together.

He was not sure. He had just started his sound career and their reputation was starting to bubble. He spent most days listening to tunes at Papa Sam's record shop, and most evenings with his boys smoking a little weed, drinking strong lagers and planning their weekends.

Dante's mind switches back to the girl with the Dax perfumed hair, as he no longer cares about Sheila. Thankfully, he can now spend most Sunday afternoons with his daughter, Micah.

His sound man, Vince, has opened the set with his signature soul tunes – imports, jazz-funk, and a little Brit soul sound, not too much as no one wants to hear a sound play commercial tunes. Once the music reels them in, Del takes over, dropping reggae grooves so tight they changed the air and made the ravers want to take on the world, the police, the Babylon system. Then the toasters take charge. Their words, chants led by Dante, are the only news reports the ravers want. They speak of the war on the streets, the SUS laws, the need for justice for those who died in police stations, the best sounds, the weakest sound, Africa and the Rastafarian faith.

By the time the sound mellowed for the lovers – would-be lovers, temporary lovers – Dante would be in need of a good grind after a little smoke. Some girl catches his eye and they dance one, maybe two songs. And normally, he would head outside to spend time talking to Darcus, the sound leader, overseeing the money collection.

Dante has a lot of respect for Darcus. They first met at Papa Sam's, and Darcus' reputation was already part of the sound folklore. He is just over five feet tall, yet his temper and determination had felled much bigger men.

His sound, 'Master D', was started by his father in the late sixties, and after his sudden death, Darcus stood up and ran the show. His legendary status as a sound man with a serious head for business made people love or hate him. His rise to the top is explained as either as man who knows music, or a man whose temper is both quiet and deadly.

There are also whispers of his father's Spanish Town connection, some of which Dante feels is a little exaggerated. Yet he has the utmost respect for Darcus' knowledge of music, and the respect he has for the three amigos – Vince, Del and Dante – is what keeps Dante with the sound. He smiles as he remembers how Sheila would often tell him that Darcus is short-changing them.

Tonight, while he makes his way outside, a girl bumps into him. Her voice catches him off-guard as he leans in to hear her apology, and he suddenly wants to see her face. This is how he finds himself still dancing with this girl. Apart from "hi", no other words pass between them. He thinks of all kinds of lines, from the usual, "have we met before?" to, "you ever been kidnapped before?" Each feels forced, and he decides that he just wants to see if she looks as good as she feels and sounds.

He leads her outside, and the sudden cool early morning air makes the beanie grip his hand. Dante acknowledges Darcus with a slight nod of the head – the look on his friend's face tells him that she must look alright.

He leads her to a lamppost, where the orange light would allow him a good enough look. He turns, and her smile moves right through him and touches a place he does not fully recognise.

He is so surprised by his own feelings that all he can do is smile back. Eventually his voice, a softer version of his toasting voice, emerges.

"I'm Dante."

"I'm Marcia."

For once Dante does not want to use lines, as he does not want to risk blowing this girl off – Marcia is someone he needs to just hold. This need unnerves him. He concentrates on regaining the moment. She allows him an in by shivering slightly and he pulls her closer.

"Sorry, it's nippy out here. Best we go back inside."

"Don't you want my number?"

He smiles shyly and she reels off seven digits. Dante realises that he has no pen, and she pulls one from her tiny handbag and writes the numbers on the back of his hand.

He leads her inside, still holding her hand...

TELEPHONE LINE

Dante and Marcia spend hours on the telephone. He finds he can tell her everything and anything – about Sheila, Micah, his father's disappearance from his life, his toasting ambitions. Conversation is easy. No woman had got him to speak about himself in such a way before. She asks so many questions and then really listens, laughing with him and not at him.

He does not discuss Marcia with his amigos, or even his mother. Only Micah. He tells Micah all about Marcia without mentioning her name. He speaks mostly of her qualities, the ones he wants Micah to own as she grows up. Micah's only response is a smile and sometimes an "oh daddy."

Dante and Marcia speak every night between 8 and 9 pm – never before or after, a rule set down by Marcia, part of her "non-studying time". He paces, watching the telephone until it rings.

Two weeks have passed since their first meeting. In that time he learnt that she moved with a different crew and the blues had been an exception as she danced in hotel ballrooms, clubs and house parties. She did not drink more than ginger ale, or a martini at a push. Nor does she smoke and doesn't comment though, when he tells her that he smokes a little weed.

Marcia is going to college and working part time, studying to be a teacher or some course like that. In the two weeks he saves a few pounds and asks Marcia to the pictures. She agrees and they set the date, Friday night, 7:30. Early enough for him to get to the set at some insurance company staff 'do'. He is no longer a box boy, so he does not have to be there too early to set up.

Dante's mother asks if he was getting married as he smells as sweet as a bride and he had been getting ready since about 5 pm. Well, since midday when he went to the barbers for a trim and a shape. He's ironed three shirts, chosen two pairs of slacks and chosen a pair of jeans.

He changed twice, finally settling on a suede-fronted Gabicci zip front cardigan over a white vest, and discarding the slacks for seamed and frayed-edged jeans. He finished the look with a pair of soft black moccasins.

He can hear his mother humming the wedding march as he comes down the stairs. He tries to keep a serious face, but his mum's teasing makes him feel good.

"Mum behave, I'm only going to the pictures."

Mum stops humming long enough to enquire if he was back with Sheila?

It is Dante's turn to start humming as he plants a kiss on her cheek.

The Palace is a fifteen-minute bus ride away. He thinks about walking, he would sweat too much. But he isn't going to chance waiting for a bus, nor can he spend any of the money he saved on a minicab. So he calls Del; his grey Hillman Imp has a tape deck and had witnessed many a late night fumble.

Del turns up, no questions asked, no real conversation and they pull up outside the Palace with ten minutes to spare. Dante stands in the foyer, checking out the patrons and the six movies on show – he is hoping for the action thriller or the comedy.

The smell of popcorn makes his stomach groan slightly. He had drunk a Guinness whilst at the barbers and eaten a packet of custard creams. He has enough money for the tickets, a couple of small popcorns and a few drinks. He just hopes she does not ask for the post-pictures burger dinner.

Dante stands with his hands in his pockets, watching the doors. She arrives on time. They smile and Dante takes her hand. They end up in an action thriller, still holding hands and sharing a box of popcorn. She jumps a few times when blood splatters the screen and he laughs, teasing her softly that she has a weak heart. She playfully punches his arm.

Dante feels like a third year student going out with a girl for the first time – he wants to giggle. The feeling continues as they make their way to a local burger bar where they share fries and two cups of tea. They do not talk much, do not need to, and then Dante feels an urge to kiss her. The moment passes. As a sound man, his woman has to be above reproach – supportive and well dressed, and not demonstrative; not cool.

The moment is gone. Dante looks closely at her features. They're all wrong. His girls are light skin with almost white features – Sheila has green eyes and bone straight hair; the other beanies after her all had that look. And although he does not go out with white girls, Del often teases him that he is one step away and Dante always replies: "the slave could never really love the owner with a true heart."

Marcia's skin is dark and smooth and her eyes brown with flecks of gold; they hold your attention, yet they are closed off, like she is working you out. Her lips are pink and kissable, thick and inviting.

"Why are you staring at me?"

"I'm trying to work out how I got so lucky."

Marcia looks at him through half closed eyes and then smiles slowly.

"You are not too hard on the eyes."

Dante laughs and taps the back of her hand – she is getting to him, hitting places he has buried under weed and hard lyrics. They sit and chit chat for another hour before he follows her to the bus stop and waits for her bus. It is here that they share their first kiss – lips and tongue, teasing and tasting. She misses the first bus, and the second. She pulls herself away to catch the third.

He steps away from the bus stop, a smile dancing on his lips until he sees them, two police officers in a car. They watch him as he crosses the road and he feels them watching him as he bends to slightly adjust the tassels on his moccasins. He steadies his breathing and stands up slowly. He walks easy as he knows he carries no weapon or any sensimilla. He waits for the tap on the shoulder. It comes. He stands still and looks directly at the policeman.

"Where are you going?"

"Home."

"You live near here?"

"Yes."

"Where are you coming from?"

Dante swallows and sucks his teeth.

"You watch me leave the burger bar, watch me with my girl at the bus stop and you watch me cross the road, so why the twenty questions?"

"Less of your lip sonny, and answer my question."

"I live near here and went to the pictures."

"Ok – I am sure you know what to do."

Dante looks at the policeman and then at his truncheon and decides that the dance is more important than sparring with some Babylon. He raises his arms and the policeman begins scanning his body with his hands, paying close attention to Dante's crotch and ankles – he is so close that Dante can smell the fish and chips he must have had for dinner, accompanied by a slight musky scent.

Dante says nothing and once he gets the 'be careful' speech, he goes home to change.

That night he smokes two big heads and drinks several Brews whilst chanting to a militant beat. He dances with a few girls, paying no mind to what their bodies promise.

He wakes up the next morning next to a beanie that snores, and had done things to him that he had only dreamed about. He steps over her, pulls on his clothes and walks through the front door.

When he gets home he feels the need to scrub the policeman and the beanie off him. He sits in the hot bath scented by Dettol, scrubbing every inch of his body with a wash cloth.

His mother knocks on the bathroom door and enters before he can say "Come in."

"Mum, the door."

"Some girl name Marcia called and said call her tomorrow as she is out tonight. She sounds nice, who is she?"

"Just a friend mum."

"Sheila was just a friend and look what happen."

"Mum."

"I know, I am minding my own business, just don't bring your business to my door."

By the time he finishes his Sunday dinner, he has decided to try a different tact with Marcia. He can wait, and when he needs a little fix there is always a beanie or two who will give him a place to rest his head.

RADIO TIME

Darcus calls Dante before noon on Monday; he is holding a special meeting. Dante does not ask why, he just meets his boys at Maria's Cafe.

"Ras clart, it must be serious, Del's here before me!" exclaims Dante on seeing Vince, Del and Darcus, their heads close together and their faces animated. None of them respond to his joke. He does not need telling, he sits down and only then does Darcus acknowledge his presence.

"Where you disappeared to Sunday morning?" Darcus asks, looking straight at Dante, who resists the urge to answer with another joke, as something in Darcus' manner makes it clear that this is no time for foolishness.

"With some beanie," Dante shrugs.

"Well, while you were getting your jollies, Rodigan was at the set. He heard you and our Water Pumpie rhythm and he wants us on his show."

Dante stares at Darcus, then at Vince, and then at Del. All three look serious. Dante sits back, closes his eyes, and sees himself performing on a stage – the noise and the beanies. Then he sees Marcia, and just like that he opens his eyes.

"Did you hear me D-boy? We're going national!"

Darcus slaps Dante's shoulder, and on cue, all four men start laughing.

Darcus orders teas and full English breakfasts all round. The group do not speak until they are at Papa Sam's record store. A move like this means finding another rhythm to blend with the 'Water Pumpie' beat. It has to be something rare – Dante can hear it, he just has no name for it.

The scratchy back beat is the only thing that reminds him of his father, a man whose features he shares but whose voice he tries not to remember. The man who, one morning, "went to buy some fags," (his mother's words) and, "kept on walking."

The scratchy seven-inchers were among the few things he left behind that Dante's mother did not throw out. Dante would play them on his little portable record player. Sometimes he would sing along, but most times he would just sit and listen to the music – each instrument, each riff, rhythm, drum snares and beat. He got so good that he could identify a band, an artiste before the first lyric as he knew each note, each instrument.

His English teacher, Mr Brookes, often told him, "If you applied your writing skills with your pencil tapping skills, you could easily end up as a famous composer."

Dante *did* take his advice. He combines his English C.S.E. grade 1 skills, and his love of music, to be a toaster, with lyrics that often leave his opponents speechless.

By the time Dante calls Marcia, he is hyped about the radio show.

"Hey Marc, what's up? Guess who's going to be on Rodigan's show?"

He has run his mouth for a good ten minutes before he realises that Marcia has been silent.

"Marc?"

"Yes…"

"You not excited for me? Do you know what this will mean?"

"Dante," her voice is soft, yet he feels something bad is about to be said, and before he can cut her off, she says it: "I'm happy for you Dante and I know you'll do well, I got to go now, goodnight."

He is still searching for the right come-back when he hears his mother asking if he is still on the phone as she has to call Betty.

Marcia is turning into a piece of work and he has no patience for all that she promises. Yet, he still wants to get to know her …

really know her. The intensity of the feeling makes him want a little weed.

He leaves his home without telling his mother where he is going. He has enough money on him to get a couple of Brews and a bag of herb, and he knows the one place where he can really enjoy all of this is by Del – no talking needed. The weed would help him reason and give him back his level line.

As usual, Del is home in his room surrounded by pictures of Bob Marley, Peter Tosh and Big Youth. Against another wall are stacks of 7-inch and 12-inch records in wooden crates that he had found outside pubs.

On the opposite wall stands his chest of drawers where each toiletry item stands neatly to attention – nothing is ever out of line. Del's bed is made up, almost priest-like. Dante and the others agree that his spell in a secure unit has left a mark.

Dante has never really asked Del about the Unit, only once when they had smoked some exceptional Jamaican herb – it had loosened their minds enough to admit how afraid they are; afraid of becoming like their fathers working in some factory. Dante remembers Del stating that if he had to go back inside the Unit he would die. The moment passed, and emotions rose with the smoke and smothered any need to acknowledge it.

Tonight though, Dante has Marcia on his mind. A woman like none of the other beanies, or even Sheila – she is demanding more of him, without actually asking for anything.

Del does not ask why Dante has come over; he just sets about rolling the Rizla paper in which lay a slim line of brown weed and a few seeds.

Once it is ready Del hands it to Dante, who lights it and for a second watches the paper start to burn. The tip turns red. He puts it to his lips and pulls, filling his lungs.

Dante closes his eyes and follows the trail of the smoke within. It goes into his lungs, then up his throat and escapes through his nostrils. Somewhere in between this scent, a memory travels into his brain and opens a draw marked 'Dad'. Dante tries to kick it shut and succeeds – jerking his foot and frightening Del.

It is Del's shouting, "I cool, I cool," that opens Dante's eyes.

He hands Del the Rizla – back and forth it goes until Dante laughs.

"My father's dead ... seen!"

Someone else is laughing; someone else is in the room. Dante doesn't really care who it is, as long as it is not his father.

Dante takes one more pull. This time he is standing on a gravel road. It is real warm and he needs something to eat, something like his mother's curry goat and rice.

"Do people really eat goats?"

The question comes from the goat standing next to him. Dante reaches out to stroke him and ends up feeling his own face.

He soon falls asleep. He dreams of nothing, and forgets about his father. He wakes up feeling even hungrier. His eyes quickly scan the room and he sees Del perched in a corner, hugging his knees and rocking slightly.

"Bwoy, Del, this stuff good. What you got to munch on?"

Del does not respond; he just keeps rocking slowly. Dante is not too concerned. Del has developed this habit lately, and normally comes around within a few. Dante leaves his friend. He leaves the ashes in the ashtray, opens the bedroom window and lights one of Del's incense sticks.

He finds a packet of crisps on the floor by the door and checks the flavour – cheese and onion.

Dante finds that he still has the need to talk. There are things in his head that are taking up too much space. He shrugs off this need, as he does not deal with feelings – nope, he is a sound-man. He breathes lyrics and the beat.

He leaves Del and after saying goodbye to Mrs Morris, he goes through the front door.

Three hours later, his mum is standing at his bedroom door. Dante hears her sobs before he understands what she is saying.

"Del's dead – Lord, Del kill himself – oh mercies – Del gone…"

Dante cannot move. His mouth is sealed, sealed like his memory of their last weed together, sealed like his fear that Del may have asked him for help, sealed like his childhood. No tears; his mother's would serve as his own.

He does not call Marcia, as he has no words to explain why Del took his own life. News of Del's death moves though the sound fraternity, but his suicide is never mentioned. His funeral will be at the All Saints Church of England, where Del, Dante and eleven other guys from St Marks School for Boys had sung in the choir, attended Sunday school and been confirmed at the age of eleven.

When they assemble for Del's funeral, Dante escorts Mrs. Morris into the small chapel. The coffin is open, and a chalky version of his friend lies inside. Del's lips are slightly parted, like he is about to say something. It is the stillness, the total stillness that holds Dante transfixed.

The service passes, fleeting with the occasional wail from Mrs Morris, who sits surrounded by a gaggle of church sisters – professional mourners who do not allow Del's friends to touch her.

The guys shuffle past the coffin, all of them dressed in black suits, white shirts with black ties. Their shoes shine – the only colour comes from their gleaming sovereign rings. As they file past, they nod at Mrs Morris. Only Dante stands in front of her long enough for her to look up at him and see the tears forming in his eyes.

He glimpses Marcia as they leave the church. She nods and he responds likewise. He does not see her again.

Dante helps to carry his friend's coffin. He cannot acknowledge that the body inside is Del.

The lowering of the coffin into the ground passes with only one heart-stopping event: somehow the rope tangles around Dante's ring. He feels himself being pulled, like Del is trying to take him on one more run.

Dante doesn't know how the rope untangles, or if he really hears Del's voice say, "It's cool."

He does know, however, that the sound of dirt hitting the wooden coffin-lid and the low moans from the church sisters will haunt him for many nights.

By the time Dante falls into his bed, he is too wired to sleep. He is angry. At first he thinks he is angry with Del for killing himself, but by the turning of the dawn, he knows he is mad with himself for being there and not seeing that his brethren needed help. The tears that had failed to fall all day come down now, soaking his pillow and washing away what was left of his youth.

RIDE THE RHYTHM

Darcus rides them hard. Their live appearance on the 'Rodigan Show' would be a major coup for the sound – live and direct not just across London but also in Kingston, Jamaica.

Dante is throwing down lyrics like a man possessed. His voice grows stronger, his chat style faster as he describes life in 'Babylon', of 'black marias', 'SUS' and beanies.

He also wants to look good. This actually makes no sense as he will be on radio, yet he has this need to look real sharp. The upcoming radio date consumes him all hours of the day – so much so that he packs away any feelings he may have for Marcia, and even Micah has only small pieces of him bound up in teaching her his new rhymes.

For the first time since leaving school he buys exercise books and pencils, and writes down lines. Lines become paragraphs, some too long to chant.

The night before their appearance, they meet at Darcus' house. Unlike the others he bought a place, and lived with Wendy, a red skin woman with long, straight 'good' hair and a civil service job. She hardly comes to the dances and she very rarely speaks to the guys.

They congregate in the kitchen, and although it smells of food none is offered; instead they drink Brews and munch on nuts. Once they are settled, Darcus gets down to the business at hand and speaks directly to Dante.

"So what lyrics do you have for us?"

Dante smiles slowly and pulls out an exercise book.

"Meet Dante's lyrical inferno – I got rhymes that will make them wild."

Vince laughs loudly and slaps Dante's back.

Darcus' face is unmoved.

"So you say, don't forget ah who sound this is – don't be running off your mouth about who you is and act like we support you. This is my sound, my money and we all reach, you understand."

Dante feels a little cold, like someone had blown cold air on his neck. He shrugs off the feeling and smiles at Darcus.

"Course D, this is all about the sound. I just a put down lyrics, you select, Vince mixes and Del, Del ah guide us, Jah know."

His words appear to soothe the lovers. Darcus responds with a smile and Vince takes two sips of his Brew. All three men nod their heads; it is a done deal.

They talk for two more hours, and it is only as Dante approaches his home that he realises that Darcus did not comment on his lyrics. Lyrics shaped by his memory of his last ride, last spliff with Del.

The noise from within the house greets him as he pushes open the door. Micah is sniffling, and his mum is quarrelling with a man. She is laying into him word by word. Dante stands on the door step, not sure if he should go in or go away, until he hears the man's voice. For a second or two he thinks he is listening to a recording of his own voice. Then he remembers being on a bike, being pushed by a man, and that man telling him how he would grow up to be a great cyclist.

He holds his breath and retreats through the front door. He does not want to see that man. His mind turns to Del. He misses him.

He buys some 'Brew' and a pack of cigarettes and heads over to the cemetery. All his bravado almost leaves him as he looks at the heavy, locked gates. Yet, he just wants to talk to Del. He checks the top of the walls for broken glass or some other deterrent and finds none. He places the cans on the wall and pulls himself up, and lands on a soft mound of earth. His eyes take a little while to adjust to the dark. He sits for a little while on a smooth, white tomb, sips a Brew and lights his first cigarette.

He looks around and sees that some of the headstones lean like old people queuing up in the post office waiting for their pensions. He scans the ground and the longer he looks the more familiar the cemetery becomes, and he remembers that Del lies in the new section with a few white crosses. He makes his way and sits next to the uneven mound.

He lights another cigarette, and opens a second can of Brew and pours a little by Del's head. The tears come softly, followed by a burning in his chest; a sound is fighting to be released. It is a sound he does not recognise. It makes his chest heave up and down, he struggles to inhale his cigarette and every sip of his Brew tries to choke him as the tears keep flowing. The longer he sits there the clearer the dark becomes, and so do his thoughts.

He knows that he does not want to see that man – his mother's ex-husband – nor does he want to hear him say, "I am proud of you." No, he is going to show that man how to love a child; Micah will know that Dante is more than a sound or a memory.

Dante puts his key in the lock and eases the front door open. The house is in darkness, accompanied by the muffled sounds coming from his mother's bedroom – the low murmuring of her radio, some sort of news station that she listens to night and day. When he was younger he thought his mother's room was a magical place, filled with friends that only she could see. This memory makes him smile.

Micah is asleep on her bed, arms flung across both pillows. He still cannot work out how someone so small could take up a whole bed. In the morning he will take her to the park and buy her a jelly doughnut – she likes that – and then he will teach her his new lyrics. He loves the way she looks at him like he is some sort of classroom teacher. Yeah, he will show his old man how to be a father.

RING THE BELL...

By the time Dante comes down for breakfast the next morning, his mother has prepared thick, creamy porridge with scrambled eggs and toast to follow.

"You should open a café, you'd make a fortune!"

His mum laughs, and Dante can see how lovely she is: big brown eyes, even teeth and lips. Full lips, just like his. People often say that when he smiles he becomes the image of his mother and that this will make him lucky.

Dante hugs his mum, and inhales her powder, sweat and frying scent. He holds her until the boy in him relaxes and the man in him becomes grounded, and she does not push him away.

He sits down to breakfast and they fall into a conversation about her day ahead. She does not ask about the radio show, like it will jinx the whole experience. Dante glances at the clock on the kitchen wall and sees that it's only 8 o'clock – only half an hour has passed since he sat down.

By 8:50 he is at the barber's, sitting and waiting his turn, rehearsing his lyrics in his mind. He picks up a newspaper and begins incorporating the headlines into his repertoire.

When the barber's sheers stop, it is Dante's cue to ease into the chair. He says nothing; Raz has been his barber for over two years and he knows that Dante likes a number '2' with an outlined hair line, trimmed side burns, goatee and pencil thin moustache.

Next stop Sully's Menswear – he needed a new Italian top and slacks, even though he would not be seen by the listeners.

Passions Shoe shop has fine Italian shoes made from the softest and most exotic skins from crocodile to ostrich. He tries on several before he settles on a pair of snakeskin with a delicate gold chain across the front. They were easy and stylish – he hates anything too flashy or loud.

Since the night in the cemetery he has stayed away from Brews and weed, and there is enough change in his pockets and on the dresser to buy his mum a box of her favourite chocolates, and a few treats for Micah from the corner shop.

No one is home. Dante leaves the chocolates on the kitchen table, takes a pack of biscuits from the bread bin, heads to the living room and watches children's programs until his eyes decide that he needs a rest.

He does not dream. No sound, just a comfortable feeling, and that is how the rest of the day feels, even when helping his mum unpack her shopping and playing with Micah. Conversations flow from one topic to another, a little teasing, a little disagreement, yet everything connects like an easy reggae rhythm and nothing disturbs his flow.

He is grateful that his mother does not mention whether or not she heard him leave, or what his father wanted. They move around each other allowing the secret to shield them from saying out loud what needs to be acknowledged.

His evening preparations began with his hot bath regime – scrubbing, soaking, inspecting and slathering every inch of his body in a thick, cold cream.

He inspects his face – not a mark or spots. The girls love his smooth skin. His secret: baby soap and Vaseline. This is a trick taught to him by his grandmother and followed from the age of seven, and he has never deviated from this. Other things like "mind your lesson" and "go to church" had long been confined to ether of his mind, however, the baby soft skin – that was a treasure.

Dante dresses slowly, careful not to crease anything. One more check in the mirror and the final touch – a splash of cologne.

His mother is sitting in the front room watching TV with the box of chocolates on her lap, Micah curled up next to her. They both look up as he stands in the doorway." You getting married?

24

You smell sweet like a bride." His mother's standard phrase every time he went out.

Dante smiles. He loves when his mother is laughing and teasing him. He walks over to his mum and stands in front of her, turning left and then right until she shoos him away. He picks up Micah, careful not to let her crease his clothes. She squirms, giggling, and Dante gives her a quick hug.

"Daddy nice!"

"Thanks girls, daddy gonna reach for the stars tonight."

"I'm so proud of you."

Those words reach him like a whisper. He follows the sound. His eyes rest on his mother, who is studiously watching the TV. He puts Micah down, bends and plants a kiss on the top of his mother's head.

The guys all stand in the foyer of one of the most famous radio stations in the UK, all dressed in their finest – Darcus and Vince in dark suits and silk shirts, with sovereign rings and double chaps gleaming. The receptionist openly stares at them, trying to figure out if they are famous. They do not acknowledge her, nor do they feel out of place.

"Dis is it, one time, one chance, they go hear us in London, back ah yard, we ah go large." And on and on Darcus rambles, his sentences getting shorter and shorter the more hyped he becomes. Vince nods. Dante stands still, feeling the lyrics move through him.

"D, D look at me, your lyrics will either make or break us; seen?"

Dante nods, but won't let Darcus' words spoil his rhythm – there is a tingling that starts at the tip of his fingertips that led to a sensation in the pit of his stomach. Then comes the call.

Sixty minutes later they were back in the same foyer, except this time Dante is doing all the talking.

"Jamaica, London – we bus dem – we gone clear, did you hear Rodigan? Did you hear the callers? And we mash up every riddim. No beanie could ah make me feel so good, man. Man, that was solid. How many riddims did we ride, three, four, ten? I don't know where dem lyrics come from; everything just come together, like rice and peas on a Sunday afternoon."

He laughs and turns to see why there is no other sound – Darcus is looking at him like he has stolen the jam from the middle of the doughnut.

"What's up?"

"Whose sound system is this?" This time Darcus' voice has a slight edge.

"Yours D, everyone knows that!"

"So why you chat so much?"

"Wha?"

"You heard me; act like you is the only one who can chat to the mic. You wanna take over my sound? You wanna pay me back every penny I give you to blow on weed and Brew, ya wotless youth."

It is the force of his words and not what he actually says that blows through Dante's mind. He looks past Darcus at the well lit tower blocks, whose brightness appear to be mocking him. He glances at Vince. He actually looks afraid.

Dante's fingers flex as he feels the joy slipping away. He needs a spliff, a big one. He needs Del and he really wants peace – he needs to walk, just walk away.

He turns his back on Darcus and heads towards the door, head held high and with a positive bounce. He feels a hand on his shoulder just as he touches the door, and turns to see a half smiling Darcus.

"No need to walk, we came together, we leave together."

Dante shrugs and the three men leave. Just as they reach Darcus' car, he feels a blow between his shoulder blades – his face hits the pavement. Darcus bends down and whispers, "Nobody takes this from me, nobody. The street is where you belong."

He blacks out. When he comes to, there is an old lady whose face is filled with horror, a look mirrored by her ratty dog. Dante wants to laugh, and he thinks he is.

FROM BOX BOY...

Sound men carry large black boxes into a three-storey house of the Kingsland High Road. Each box is designed and built by Wills, one of the best sound men in east London. Boxes are placed on each of the three floors, and he gets the guys to place them slightly side on to the room so that the sound would cover the whole room without distorting its true sound.

Wills wires all the boxes to the DJ's console, and places a telephone receiver to his head and listens to the record playing on the first deck. He cues the record on the second deck, listens for the exact beat to align themselves and delays the start of the second track for a few minutes so that the two beats would meld seamlessly into each other.

Tonight, he is not the main attraction. That honour belongs to Dante, a guy from south of the river – a young blood who rocked Rodigan's show a few months back.

The word is that this guy's lyrics flow as easy as honey over hot toast. His face makes the beanies stand close. Yet, he has the ugliest scar. It starts at the base of his hairline and disappeared below his collar. Some say he crossed some 'Sticksman', others say some beanie's man caught him in their bed. He never talks about it.

This Dante wears polo neck jumpers under his Italian cardigans. It is said that he speaks very little between sets and then he runs his lyrics like a modern day Shakespeare – lyrics deep, rhythmic and one step ahead of all the others. He quoted scriptures regularly and chat 'bout Del, the angel of St Mark's.

It is another three hours before the rave gets under way, and the homeowners are making sure that their valuables are locked away. Someone, must be one of their mums, is busy lifting pot covers, stirring contents and occasionally complaining about the heat in the kitchen. And yet, she does not leave this space. The smell fills the space between the walls and the speaker boxes.

HONEY LIPS...

R hythms slide into each other, enticing the ravers to move their impassive exteriors – it is not cool to show enjoyment. The DJ knows that he has them when there is no murmuring, just cigarette smoke and swirls of weed.

Women with immaculate hairstyles and fur coats wait for the touch on the arm – she will turn, he will put his arms around first her waist and then, depending on the intensity of the lyrics, he will pull her closer and slow the rhythm until it looks as if they are one.

By the time Dante arrives behind the mic, the crowd is primed. His opening lines send an electric charge through the room. Guys suspend their quiet, sexual advances, and women will turn and stare. This is the moment Dante loves. He can feel the power as he chants, "Jah is my guide," and there is a collective response of, "Jah Rastafari." He then pays tribute to his fallen soldiers: Colin Roach, who died in a police station in Stoke Newington, and Del. For Dante, their spirits stand beside him and help to ease the tension.

For a few hours, he is riding the rhythm. It was a few weeks ago that he realised that, like a preacher, he could start a call and response – no more silent changes. Now they sing back to him. They feed him, force him to read more books, biographies, newspaper articles, the Bible. He then spends hours listening to records, beats and lyrics. He even started picking singles with his eyes closed and rhyming within the first ten beats.

Tonight, he seals his reputation as a stand-alone DJ, no longer a member of a sound – he will be invited by club owners, dance promoters and sounds to be a guest DJ. He has learnt that his scar gives him a certain amount of kudos and allows him to be quiet, only speaking when he has the mic in his hand. He hears the rumours of how he got the scar. No one mentions Darcus or the severing of his brotherhood.

His mother no longer asks what happened the night the police found him bleeding on the sidewalk outside a tube station. She had tried as he lay silently in the hospital bed, and she tried as the police officers asked him over and over if he knew his assailants. She asked the night he tried to put his fist through a pane of glass. If she knew anything, she never said.

Marcia had visited him once. Her eyes filled with fear, and she did not come close to the bed. Her aloofness pissed him off.

His stay in hospital allowed him to formulate his revenge during the long silences between meal and visiting times. Vince came once, clutching a bag of grapes, which Dante hates, and a newspaper, which he appreciated. Neither mentioned the night Rodigan made them famous. Rodigan had sent a basket of fruit and a note about standing 'firm'. His mother gave him a Bible.

He takes all these things with him when he toasts. At first he wanted to cover the scar, and even thought about growing his hair long. He wore polo necks instead. Then one night a beanie touched his scar tenderly and spoke of 'how hard" it made him. He also noticed that the other sound guys would be more direct with him and will pay him his money without squabbling. It was then that Wills, aka the Professor, his favourite engineer, told him about the various stories about how Dante got his scar, and the root statement, "Honey lips has tasted death."

Dante liked the words so much that when a producer asked him about putting his lyrics on vinyl, 'Honey Lips' was the first track he put down in a poorly lit studio in north London. The producer added a young singer by the name of Jerome Matthews, who changed his name to J. Matthew – London Silk. 'Honey Lips' became a club and party favourite, and soon they were making personal appearances at various clubs in and outside of London.

And after every club date he returns to his mother's house, placing the cash on the kitchen table before going to bed. At around 5 pm, his mother will wake him and there'll be some money on his bedside cabinet.

He also gives money to his daughter's mother, who is less hostile, although occasionally she gave women at the dances and parties where he was playing the impression that they were still together. Her current boyfriend got fed up with her behaviour and warned her to stop. Dante doesn't care, one way or the other, what she does or says, as long as she leaves Micah with him.

Dante still smokes weed, often alone in his room – it calms him. But these days, he wears expensive Italian knitwear and Cecil Gee suits. His shoes are made of the softest, exotic animal skins and he adorns his neck and wrists with thick, heavy gold pieces. He still has his hair and beard trimmed by the same barber. He no longer eats breakfast in cafes.

And every Thursday morning, he goes to the churchyard and sits or stands by Del's grave. Sometimes he will tell Del about his latest gig and late night running. Talking with Del gives him a level line. Occasionally, there were other mourners, mainly old ladies with small bunches of flowers.

At first they eye him suspiciously and clutch their handbags. Gradually, they get used to seeing him. Once or twice they would mutter something about the weather or the outrageous cost of flowers.

Dante never brings flowers for Del. Once, he placed a small bag of weed under the flower arrangement left by Del's mum. Usually, he smokes a big head and blows the smoke over the headstones as if Del can inhale.

He does not tell Del about Darcus' betrayal and Vince's weakness. He deals with that alone. On Thursdays, after leaving Del, he feels stronger and verbally charged. He goes home, straight to his room, and begins writing lyrics, sometimes too long to chat on a mic and sometimes too personal to be shared. He keeps these in another folder marked 'Micah'.

The rhythm of his life flows nicely. The appearances are growing. Rodigan plays his 'Honey Lips' track often and hails him as the new king of fast chat. Dante drops his faux Jamaican accent as his naturally fast London cadence feels real; it gets a great response from the ravers. He speaks like them and about the things they see every day: black marias, the SUS laws, casual people, beanies and Babylon – east and south London idioms over a fast, smooth delivery. Soon, other toasters are doing the same. It is now cool to be a black Londoner.

Dante is riding the rhythm; he no longer thinks about what he does not have. It is all about the mic – toasting. His 'Micah' folder fills up with conversations with Del, his ol' man, Micah and his mum. These pieces cannot be shared; they are too close to his heart, and for now, the scar serves as a reminder and a shield.

25 LESSONS

The one day Dante lets down his guard is his birthday. His mum never asks him what he wants or how many friends he wants to come over. Nope, it's their day.

A few days before, the house fills with the smell of baking. Then she covers the dark, rich fruit rum cake with thick, royal icing, and decorates it simply with his name in light blue icing and a single candle. Only once had she run out of blue colouring – the cake that year had been blank and he had cried, not believing the cake was for him.

For years the ritual began with him waking up to a gift and card placed on the bedside cabinet, followed by a full, cooked breakfast no matter what time of the day he got up. And they always sat together, and he showed his mum his gift as if it was the first time she had seen it. His mum would be all excited and involved, and would want to know how it worked; how it fit; how it smelt. Then she would bring out the birthday cake with its glowing candle, singing the birthday song in her high-pitched voice. He would smile, close his eyes and then blow out his candle as his mum insisted that he make a wish.

This would be followed by clapping and cake-cutting and Dante eating a healthy slice or two; birthday done. Once Micah came on the scene, she would occasionally become a part of the ritual, as excited as her father about the "pretty cake" and burning candles.

This year was not going to be any different. Nope. He has an all night blues dance the night before, but he will make sure that he is home by 9 am. It would mean a fast drive down the motorway – on a Sunday – so no worries about traffic or even police. He knows his mum will be up and waiting, red beans cooking on the fire. Micah will be there as well.

The all-nighter is in Blackpool, a seaside town some five hours' drive from London; a trip involving seventeen coaches filled with young, urban black Londoners ready to spend pennies in the arcades and scream on roller coasters and bumper cars, then buying sticks of rock before dancing until the small hours.

The police are there to welcome the coaches as they drive along the main road. Locals gawk at the arrivals, instinctively clutching their handbags, their poodles and their wallets. Some shake walking sticks at the laughing black faces, whilst others stand and speak to their neighbour.

The day passes without a hitch. Dante even manages to meet a young lady who reminds him of Marcia in looks. She does not ask as many questions, though. It makes him feel better as he has allowed Marcia to slip from his life – no calls, or glimpses at parties or dances. In his present state of being, he does not need a woman who will make him feel like he needs to do more.

The organisers have lined up the best entertainment in London, including two solo acts; three sound systems; and an MC, a rising star on the comedy circuit who has appeared in a couple of TV shows. As Dante enters the hall, he catches a glimpse of his reflection in the entrance hallway mirror. The face looks familiar, yet there is hardness around the eyes and mouth. For a moment he sees shadows of the man who walked out of his life, and he feels he kind of understands the rage that made men walk away. He instinctively touches his scar.

He deposits the beanie at a table near to the stage and makes his way back-stage, where he nods to the others and takes his place in a dark corner. It allows him to hear the music, inhale the sensimilla being shared by the other sound men, and be still. He runs a set of lyrics through his mind whilst waiting his turn. The words "hustler" and "love" keep coming back. A rhythm teases him, and then he hears it: Jimmy Cliff's 'The Harder They Come'.

He is ready. When his turn comes, he turns the dance upside down. The ravers move closer to the stage and he rules them with rhyme and rhythm. Words flow from him and fill the space between stage and raver. He does not look at anyone; he is talking to Del, his dad, all those who have left him. He tells the men to be strong and stand firm and the women to love them, for mothers to hug their sons. He feels powerful, like the Holy Ghost giving strength to the disciples. By the time he steps away from the mic, the MC declares that Honey Lips Dante is the number one DJ in the UK.

He steps back into the shadows, feeling rather than hearing the congrats. He looks for his beanie, she is still sitting at a table. As he walks towards her, he hears a sound so familiar that a chill runs down his spine. His next instinct is to run away from that sound. There is a scream, shouting, whistles and feet running on concrete, and someone shouts, "He went that way!"

Dante looks behind him and sees a man lying on the floor with two guys kneeling beside him. One has wrapped his jumper around the gushing wound. He hears one of the guys say, "You alright, you alright? Somebody call an ambulance, now!"

A guy in a trench coat bumps into Dante hard enough to spin him sideways and leaves a wet stain on the front of his Italian-knit jumper. In no time, the police – complete with angry dogs – are on the scene, long before the ambulance. Young men instantly become wary with closed-mouth determination, already planning their own brand of justice on the young man who has sliced one of their own.

Hours after the police finally let them leave Blackpool, Dante hears that the victim is one of the junior DJs. Michael, a kid from east London who was being touted as the next big thing. The rumours travel from coach to coach that he died, over a woman/coat/lyrics. Women cry openly and young men shake their heads. nNo one speaks above a whisper. By the time they reach London, it has become clear that the young man lives.

Dante's new lady lays her head on his shoulder, but her softness cannot mask the memory of the blade slicing his neck. He hopes that Michael will rise from this stronger and in need of no one but himself. The beanie stirs and Dante pats her thigh. She moves closer and he wonders if she lives alone...

TWO INTO ONE DON'T GO

Nights and shows roll into one. Dante is back in the studio with one of the female lovers rock singers, whose distinct alto voice has moved from the smoky blues dances to the national pop charts. Her label decides that the 'B' side needs to feature a toasting track, and they want Dante. The label also asks for his manager's name – he blurts out his mother's name, as she handles all his money and often takes messages whilst he sleeps.

This studio is near to his home, a cool walk that takes him past the old café where Darcus had told them about the Rodigan show. The session lasts all night and his lyrics change slightly with every take. He finds the song lyrics a little simple, yet the ravers love it, so he hangs a strong hook around the chorus, a reply to her question, "Why?" He finds himself thinking of Micah's mother and he asks in response to her, "Why wasn't he good enough, man enough to be with her?"

The producer nods, the singer brushes away a tear and Dante feels a light moving through his heart, brightening the dark corners where Del and his father's memories lay.

He steps out of the gloom of the studio to the slightly brighter morning sky – he squints whilst trying to catch his bearings. He is hungry, and fancies a fry up with all the works, but the nearest spot is Darcus' spot. He tells himself that it is too early for Darcus to be there. Even if he sees them, he has nothing to say; the scar has healed. He pours most of his anger into his lyrics, and it fuels his growing career. He slips inside the café and is met by the wet, steamy heat of builders and old men reading the racing pages.

He makes his way to a corner that allows him to face the door. A woman with a grey, wet cloth wipes the table and takes his full breakfast order with a small pot of tea.

He feels he is being watched. He looks up and sees Vince peering in. He nods. Vince nods back, and hesitates before walking off. Dante dismisses this encounter and concentrates on eating his hot, full breakfast – fat sausages, strips of streaky bacon, two fried eggs with bright yellow centres, baked beans, fried tomatoes, mushrooms and thick slices of white bread. He ate each item like a man tasting it for the first time.

The record's reissue, with Dante's toasting 'B' side, speeds up the national pop charts and Rodigan, as well as every sound system and the top national radio station, calls it the sound of Black British youth.

Dante's mother rose to the challenge of being his manager even though she did not attend any of his sessions. She ensures that he gets paid up front for the full amount requested and she made sure that his clothes and shoes are clean and ready. She curbed his gold buying habit with one sentence: "Nice girls will not be impressed by all that gold."

She also finds out about making sure his name appears as the writer. He has no idea how important that is, until one day his mum hands him a cheque marked "royalties" – he laughs.

His performance schedule was cranking up with a couple of radio appearances. And then it comes – the call to perform with the female lovers rock singer, whose song 'Why?' is now a national hit, on a television music show.

Dante thinks his mother has taken down the message wrong, and it is the studio producer's call – his voice rumbling down the line talking of rehearsals, pick up times, wardrobe – that makes him realise that he is really going be on TV. All he could say is, "Thank You."

He punches the air and runs into the kitchen, where his mother and daughter sit at the table with looks of unabashed pride. It catches him off guard and tears prick his lashes. He shakes them off before he plants wet kisses on mum's cheek. He doesn't want to touch her as it would make the tears fall down; there is sadness there so deep he is afraid to let it out. He picks up Micah and hugs her.

This new gig adds two new dimensions to Dante's life – rehearsals and interviews. People want to hear about him, and not just his lyrics. His private schedule is now public, he feels like he was back in school, and he does not enjoy having his words rewritten by strangers who dwell on his home life, schooling and his music. He also does not like rehearsing, having to deliver the same lines over and over.

Dante walks off the stage two hours into his first full rehearsal. "This not real – my words come from Jah and you can't tell Jah when and how he a go talk!"

No one follows him outside, and he stands with his hands in his pockets and lets the cool air smooth his inner heat. He finds himself thinking of Marcia, and wants to speak to her. The feeling disappears as fast as it appeared; they had only spoken a couple of times since Del's death.

He finds that no one questions him and he takes to the centre of the floor. The DJ cues the track, the singer sings her two opening verses and Dante rolls in with new lyrics, teasing the audience with lines. He is singing some lines and fast chatting others.

His mum smiles more, yet appears to be growing slimmer. At first he thinks she has changed her style of dressing, until one morning on his way to bed after another night session. He catches a glimpse of her checking her neck in the living room mirror, and he can see her veins. He says nothing, yet finds himself inspecting her and notices the dark circles under her eyes. Whenever she sees him looking at her she shoos him away. One day she drops a pot of water. Luckily it was cold water. Micah's scream woke him up.

The ambulance takes an eternity to arrive and it takes all his strength not to bawl – he soothes Micah whilst cradling his mother, whose moist, shallow breath is the only sign that she is still with him.

The ambulance crew pull him away and set about speaking to his mother in that detached, 'do you speak English' tone, asking her to open her eyes. One of them asks Dante for her name. For a split second he wants to say, "Mum" but stops himself in time and says, "Daphne." Saying her name makes him feel disrespectful.

They let him and Micah sit in the ambulance as they race to the local hospital. They join the throng of sick persons in casualty. She is still semi-conscious, and Dante stands holding her hand while Micah clings to him.

A young white man with spiky, yellow hair opens the curtains, calls his mother's name, and skims his eyes over her whilst scribbling on a pad. Dante asks questions and each one is met with a "she'll be ok now she's here" and "we'll run some tests and have her home in no time."

By the third such answer, Dante drops his mother's hand and strides towards the young man. It was Micah's plea of "No daddy" that stops him from slapping the smugness off his white face.

"I just want to know what's wrong with my mum and her name is Daphne, not her, not she, but Daphne."

The young doctor's face reddens and sweat beads pop on his forehead.

"I'm sure it's nothing to worry about, just calm down and a nurse will be in to see her, I mean Daphne, soon."

When Dante turns to look at his mother he sees a faint smile flicker across her lips and he smiles back, before bending down and telling Micah that "daddy was angry with the doctor but he wouldn't hurt him."

He and Micah consume four cups of lukewarm tea, two boxes of blackcurrant juice, packs of crisps and packs of digestive biscuits while waiting for his mum to be admitted.

48 hours later, his mother declares herself better by issuing strict instructions of what he needs to bring from home.

"Go in my room and top of the wardrobe you will see my white overnight case and then go to the chemist shop and buy a bottle of Dettol, some mints and a couple of puzzle books, and bring my Bible from the bedside table."

Dante touches her slightly clammy brow and takes Micah back to her mum's before taking care of his mum's business.

The overnight case feels heavy and he peeks inside. It is full with pink and frilly things and a pair of fluffy slippers. All look new and he has no memory of ever seeing his mum in anything like this. It is like she expected to go the hospital.

When he asks her about it, she smiles and waves him off with a: "I always ready, I not getting younger and you wouldn't know what to pack."

Dante's first night home alone, he puts on every light in the house. He stands in the empty kitchen. There is no smell of food being cooked. He opens the fridge door and sees Tupperware containers of food. He opens and sniffs the contents, then eats cold chicken and rice. He sits watching the television until the test card appears, but even then his feet will not let him go upstairs to bed.

The morning finds him cold and stiff on the settee. The thud of the mail hitting the floor makes him move – he stretches and is about to call out "mum" when he remembers she is not upstairs.

Two mornings later, he makes a call. He has not rehearsed what he will say should Marcia answer. His first words are: "Can we talk?"

And for the next hour he speaks of his mum and her treatment, and Marcia does what she does best: she listens and asks questions. At the end of the conversation he feels calm enough to ask her to come over.

Marcia arrives with a shopping bag and a bouquet of flowers.

"You look awful. I know your mother spoil you, so I bought you some breakfast – well, a *hot* breakfast."

He takes the bags from her and she sets about sorting out his breakfast whilst at the same time telling him to bathe, shave and change.

"Are the flowers for me?"

She laughs. "Yeah, right."

He smiles, bounds upstairs and later comes down to a quality fry-up complete with a side dish of fried plantain. As he wipes his plate with the last slice of white bread, he notices that there is no plate in front of Marcia.

"You not eating?"

"Nope. It's like the smell's enough to fill my belly, so I'm not hungry."

"Crazy."

"I know."

Dante leans back in the chair. He wants a spliff, but Marcia has other ideas.

"Why did you stop calling me?"

He instinctively closes his eyes. For once lyrics fail him.

"I got busy."

"Who is she?"

"She? My career, my toasting, or haven't you heard the records?"

Dante can see her retreating; her eyes go flat.

"Marcia, look, I'm sorry. Listen, I thought you were not too impressed with me and my lifestyle, you go college and thing and I, I belonged to a sound."

"Did you ask me, did you ask me what I wanted?"

Dante feels deflated.

They sit in silence until Marcia leans forward and touches his cheek – this is all he needs as he gets up, pulls her to her feet and kisses her, long and hard. No resistance. He leads her upstairs – the sex is intense. It is what he has needed, human connection from someone he feels really cares for him.

They arrive at the hospital ward in time to hear Dante's mother telling a nurse's aide that she needs to add a little more Dettol to the water as it will help get rid of the 'sick people' smell.

Dante cannot hide his joy.

"Mum, rest nah."

"I'm not too sick to teach you some manners."

Dante hands her the overnight case and she smiles at Marcia.

His mother's strong voice does not hide her slightly slower movements, or the way she has to concentrate to remember what each item is. Dante can see that she is crying; he stands still and allows her to pass off her tears as something to do with the medication and the state of the bathrooms. She asks him to help her off the bed and she says 'no' to any help after that. She shuffles off, and Marcia follows a few paces behind her.

Neither woman speaks, yet Dante is sure they know that each other is there. He sits next to his mum's bed and scans the rest of the ward: shrivelled bodies the same colour as the white sheets and pillows, what he thinks could be dead bodies. He looks at the bed next to his mother's and the woman smiles, showing pink gums. He smiles back.

He is the only black, young man on the ward and the nurses comment that he is a "good boy" every time they pass.

Each two hour visit is punctuated by his mum's need to go, unaided, to the bathroom, followed by a lengthy discussion of Dante's obvious lack of cooking skills, dodgy eating habits and so-so housekeeping abilities. Marcia and his mum speak easily, like long lost friends. He has to remind them to stop ganging up on him.

After each evening visit Marcia catches a bus to his home and Dante goes to the recording studio. He has been toying with some new lyrics, ones dedicated to his mum, her love, her food, her rod of correction, her healing fingers and words that pull him along as she maps out his road to manhood. One night the rhymes just slide out of him and the engineers do not stop him. He chats about the times she greased his scalp section by section, fingers strong yet tender. He can hear her singing some Jim Reeves song every Sunday morning before she set off to church. He asks her if she loved another man, as she never spoke of his father or any other man. And he wonders if she is ever lonely. And the questions continue, a conversation he knew he will never have.

His mum's release from the hospital coincides with his first rehearsal for his upcoming live, national television performance. Marcia will keep his mother company whilst he is at the rehearsal studio. He is dressed simply, minus his gold jewellery as it keeps blinding the cameraman. At the last minute he puts on a trilby.

Any nerves he had been feeling disappear when the director points at him and the presenter, a fiery blonde in satin hot pants and Jimmy Hendrix t-shirt, introduces him – almost hysterical in tone. The mellow tones delivered by the reigning lovers rock queen calms him and he steps into the light, delivering his lyrics, riding the rhythm like a jockey on a Grand National winner. He does not need anyone to tell him how good he sounded as he could sense that the staff, mainly white, really felt him as they do their slightly off-beat jig even when the set is done. The host asks him to come on her radio show, and one of the show's dancers places a piece of paper with her telephone number in his hand.

The director tells him that if he performs like that during the live show, he is going to be huge.

He performs even better on the Thursday night show. His mum's review consisted of, "You look younger on television." Micah said that he looked "handsome," and Marcia went on about the camera loving him.

When he plays his next set upstairs of a local pub he notices a few white youths, girls mainly, looking straight at him as he takes his position behind the deck. Then it happens – he hears one of the spinners say that Dante, "feel he reach." He ignores the taunt, but when he tries to speak to one of the other DJs, he is ignored.

Now and again his mic cuts out or the track is slightly behind his cue. He jokes about it until the end of the evening, when he glimpses Darcus and Vince. The scar on his neck begins to itch. He feels the fury rising in his head. He spots an empty beer bottle close at hand and knows he could slice Darcus as easily as slicing an apple.

The three men look at each other, no words or movement. Around them, box boys are busily unplugging boxes, wrapping wires and placing records in their correct crates. Everyone is pointedly ignoring the tension in the air. It reminds Dante of his school days, when a fight is brewing and the whole school senses it and gathers in the playground to urge the first slap or punch.

It is Vince who finally makes the first step. He stands in front of Darcus with his back to Dante. His body language makes it clear that he is telling Darcus to cool it.

The moment passes. Darcus turns and makes a motion with his finger, drawing a line across his throat. Both men leave, and the hall suddenly bursts into life – people talking, boxes scraping, laughter, smoke, weed and cigarettes, and the clinking of empty glasses and cans.

All the good times he is experiencing could soon be gone, as he has to make a decision: when to face Darcus and manners him?

ROCK STEADY

Dante is playing out more, and has another television appearance booked. His producer is ready to work on an album solely made of his toasting – no covers, just original tracks by Dante. He hit the studio straight away. The back-beats are mainly reggae rhythms and a couple of dub tracks. He takes words from his own exercise books, as well as Bible quotes and bits of poems he likes.

Marcia is a constant presence most evenings, and if he has to record all night she stays with his mother and occasionally Micah.

Yet there is a sense of failure that sits behind his smile. It has dug away at him ever since he faced off with Vince and Darcus; he needs to deal with Darcus. He has never been one to carry a knife. He never felt he needed it – when he did get into a fight it was a straight punch up. His one and only cut had come from Darcus.

The need to strike back is beginning to cloud his reasoning. He tries talking to Del, and gets angry with the cold, hard tombstone as it offers no comfort or assistance. He curses Del for taking his own life.

He smokes more weed, not just when he needs inspiration. He is now smoking at his mother's house. He gives some to Marcia and she inhales too much, coughs, and spends the rest of the night munching.

His lyrics are darker. He speaks of death and the comfort of angels, he describes the feel of a blade on skin, the betrayal of a brother being more deadly than a knife to the heart, and a slow, slow and painful slide downwards.

One day Micah pulls one of his notebooks from off his shelf and leaves it open on the bed. She has covered one of the pages in purple crayon. He gets real angry, shouts at her about disrespecting his things. Her crumpled face shows him that he has hurt her.

He buys a switchblade from a youth who hangs around the chip shop. The cool steel handle makes him feel better, more in control. Its instant, silent, spring action made him giddy with excitement.

He goes over scenarios of how he can catch Darcus unaware and slice his cheek or chest.

He carries the blade everywhere, often touching it during performances like a magic stone.

His simmering anger is affecting his relationship with Marcia. He finds her questioning, followed by silences, annoying. And when she sees the blade for the first time on the night stand she starts her preaching, and for the first time, he blanks her. He can feel her pulling away and he does nothing to stop her. This is something he *has* to do; he has to let Darcus and all the others know that he is a man, not afraid to face them, not afraid to die.

This shadow starts to cover his laughter, his forward thinking. It darkens his writing and even his mother shies away from him, questioning with her eyes and her hymn signing the 'devil' under her roof.

The need to hurt Vince and Darcus makes breathing a little easier, and feeling the cold steel makes him feel stronger, in control. His plans vary from suicidal to ridiculous: attacks in dark corners; copious amounts of blood; the two men begging and squealing. It also gets in the way of his thinking, his daily writing and his weekly conversations with Del.

He finds his soldiers when he is asked to guest DJ with a sound from the Stonebridge Park Estate; the Professor is the engineer and the Antonio brothers the spin masters. They have a level vibe, and over the next four hours Dante learns they too want to stop Darcus – they do not know how they will get him, yet they are now united by the music and the blade. Dante felt their strength and it fuels his dreams. That night his voice is strong and warrior like.

But he wants to be more than a voice, a man with cash and a crisp wardrobe. He wants to be respected by the men on the street. It is time for the scar to be revealed.

One day, Marcia asks, "Why aren't you happy?"

He puts her fingers to his lips and brushes the back of them with kisses. She curls her fingers and he leans in, not letting go while brushing his lips against her neck. In this soft moment he wants to say all that is inside him, and then she goes into her history talk about men who have fought great odds, such as Malcolm X and Bob Marley, and some man in South Africa locked away in prison for just wanting to be treated as a man. He looks at her as she speaks. Her eyes are bright and her lips move quickly. Her passion arouses him and he kisses her, long and slow, until he feels her give slightly.

Then one day, she stops talking so much. He attends her graduation, where he meets her brother. Not long after, she gets a freelancing writing job and her visits become less frequent. Her excuse becomes "I got a deadline/early morning meeting/ interview", and then she announces that she is off to the Caribbean for three months, travelling to some small island to write. And then she is gone.

Dante does not try to stop her, nor does he discuss if they will continue when she returns. He does not see her off, and as he falls into bed, Marcia's flight takes off.

His world is expanding – bigger shows with bigger pay. His second television appearance on the weekly pop show gets him an interview for a teen TV show. His age, 22, does not faze the producer. Dante does not like the script, the staff or the thought of having to work every day. He says, "No."

LIGHTS, CAMERA, ACTION

There comes an offer for a role in a new film about sound men in London. The part would be filmed in two weeks, three at most. Dante wasn't much of a cinemagoer – action movies here and there, otherwise it is cartoons with and without Micah.

The film is being shot in north London, and involves the Professor and the Antonio brothers as well as a couple of lovers rock singers. Dante is being paid to be himself, a young man with dreams of being the best DJ in London.

The clothes, though of a cheaper quality than he normally wears, are as familiar as the wallpaper in the passage of his mother's house.

His audition involves looking into a camera and speaking about his school days. At first his voice is barely audible, and several times they stop filming and ask him to speak up.

He speaks for five minutes, and then waits two days before he is offered the role. His mother dances around the kitchen when he tells her, and Micah asks "if he is going to be famous". He has no idea; all he knows is that he is being paid the equivalent of at least twelve sets. He stares at the cheque for two days before handing it to his mother, who cries.

He is about to call Marcia when he remembers that she is thousands of miles away. Nor could he pass by Del's home, smoke a celebratory spliff and laugh about his movie star life. Outside of his mum and Micah there is no one to share this moment with.

He decides to go the graveyard. He buys two cans of beer and he sits by Del's tombstone. He does not speak. He can feel hot tears rolling down his cheeks, and he wipes them away; he does not want to show Del his weak side. He forces his mind to bring up the hurt and his unformed plan to pay Darcus back. Since the night with the Professor and the Antonio brothers where they made their oath, the plan has gone from a physical attack to the undoing of Darcus' reputation as a sound man.

Dante hears Del laughing, and the words 'sound clash'. Sound versus sound, track for track, lyric for lyric, DJ versus DJ. It is so damn simple that Dante starts laughing. Trust Del to cut to the chase and state it as it is. He opens a can and pours some over Del's spot – his libation – and drinks the rest.

That night he strategises on paper, writing down the names of the best guys on the circuit – guys who have felt Darcus' wrath.

The plan finally falls into place during the early days of filming. The whole movie star experience is far more involved than Dante ever imagined – learning the script, filming, the way it jumps around, the takes and re-takes. It's like being in a studio – got to do it 'til the rhythm runs right. For the first week he runs with the program, repeating the words he has learntbut never really connecting to them. At the start of the second week, one of the writers stops him before he goes onto the set. The scene starts with a killing, and the young DJs are trying to figure out how it happened.

The writer asks Dante a set of general questions, his thoughts and feelings about the story so far, and then he says, "Dante, for these next couple of scenes I want you to dig deep. Find a time when someone betrayed you so badly that you wanted to kill them."

The words burn him and he immediately thinks of Darcus. Then he remembers the man who left him to go buy a pack of fags, and passed through his mother's house fifteen years later. He thinks of Del taking his own life without telling him that he, too, was afraid. His face must have conveyed the darkness within, as the writer hurries off.

Dante carries the pain in front of the camera, and it was not until the end of the scene that he realises his co-actors have tears running down their cheeks. The director clears his throat before yelling, "Cut!"

It is then that the final plan falls into place, as he stands over his 'friend's' body. He realises that Darcus is a coward, and he does not need elaborate plans to pay him back. No knives, no traps, no words. Well, not directly. The challenge has to be made, the seed planted on the street, at the blues dances, spreading wildly until Darcus has no choice except to say, "Yes."

The film's crowd scenes involve real ravers, sound men and UB40 collectors. Dante wonders out loud, "If Darcus is so good, how come he's not here?" He shrugs his shoulders at a beanie with bulging eyes, and she cut her eyes at him. Bait taken. He has started to reel Darcus in.

After filming that day, he meets with the Professor and the Antonio brothers to outline his plan. They silently nod their heads before sealing their involvement with firm handshakes.

Next step, a visit to Papa Sam's to find the rare tunes and rhythms. It has to be all about love as he know that Darcus will expect him to come at him with warrior chants. He is gonna kill Darcus with kindness – love lyrics, biblical and physical. He is going to get the crowd singing and dancing with him.

Between filming, Papa Sam's and a couple of live performances, he sees even less of Micah. However, his mother takes care of her, and one day he realises that Micah no longer goes away. When he enquires, his mother tells him that Micah's mother is on remand for some prostitution thing, and she has stepped in and taken Micah. She even got him to sign papers – papers he never reads or asks what they were for, such is his trust of his mother. He thanks her with a hug and tells himself that he needs to take Micah to the park.

Filming is winding down. Dante finds that he is more interested in the technical side of the procedure, and hangs around with the sound technicians and cameramen and grips – he asks questions and they answer.

He is back to writing lots of words, filling exercise books with quotations, lines, sentences, no longer just lyrics – maybe a snippet of something like the stories they had read in English Literature. He is not sure where the writing is taking him and he makes sure he does not share it with anyone.

By the last day of filming the rumours have come back to him – Darcus makes it known that he does not need any film to show how good he is.

The four men meet often and practice in old church halls. They rhyme, they reason and smoke herb. They listen to rhythms so old that Papa Sam has to explain the mento beat– the slow, hypnotic, scratchy beats that speak to parts of themselves that they hid from each other. One night the memories refuse to be held down any longer, and they talk of loss of friends, loss of fathers, brothers, lovers, and the men their mothers loved who left. That night, tears wash their faces. Nobody sees, yet the pain is eased. After that, the lyrics become more political – daily injustices, police harassment, stop and search, questioning, jobs applied for and denied. Old ladies clutching their handbags as they approached them in well lit streets, the teachers who placed them in lower streamed classes that fed their apathy, the women who gave them children whilst demanding money more than love or time with them.

Dante finally writes about his fear of dying alone in the street. Fighting is one thing, but to be stabbed and left to die on a dirty sidewalk… No, he wants to die in love.

The whispers get back to him that Darcus and his sound have built new, state of the art boxes with woofers and tweeters, slim and tall with bass tops. It makes Dante smile, for this confirms that Darcus has no lyrics, no toaster worthy of facing Dante – he is going to depend on sounds. This makes Dante and his guys work harder, coaching them and testing words, phrases and music.

His mother confronts him about being too obsessed with his music and missing too much time with his daughter. He then receives a letter from Marcia all the way from the West Indies – a blue, thin airmail envelope. The paper is covered in large, loopy letters, and she writes of water, blue, crystal clear and warm; of hot days and warm nights; sounds of animals; eating hot bread with cheese or chicken sausage or salt fish, and her new love, hot corn beef; of fast moving buses crammed with people; buckets of fruit and fresh fish; and banks where all the staff are fair-skinned and white people with Antiguan accents. He can almost hear the honking horns and feel the heat on the back of his neck. He reads and rereads her letter and places it in his Bible next to a lock of Micah's hair.

He returns to the studio with a fresh momentum. Marcia is his girl, she has crept under his shield, she did her own thing and he moves forward. He pours this feeling into a new song, 'Your Eyes', and he describes her as a lioness – graceful, strong, true love like no other. He says on record what he fails to say to her privately. This is definitely a new kind of love, and on vinyl is the only way he can show what he feels.

Marcia left before he could put word to his feelings, shape them without music. Maybe words might have kept his father close and allowed Del to live.

And Darcus – the man who liked his lyrics, who paid in beer and weed money – who gave him room to live under his shadow and the minute he stepped beyond that shadow, he literally stabbed him in the back.

When he looks at his daughter, Micah, he wants to hold her and keep her at the age she is now, just hold her and tell her to forget about growing up, becoming a woman and having a man of her own or even children. He wants her to keep loving and trusting only him.

Sometimes he watches her sleep and he wants to scream out of fear. He works harder and gives his mother full control of his money, for he wants Micah to want for nothing and have a start that will make her independent, maybe even go to university. He is pushing Micah to be an achiever beyond the boundaries of the regular raves and the Coney fur coats. He talks to her in adult tones, outlining life in the real world.

He finally understands what his mother had tried to do with him. She did everything she could to keep him in school, out of prison and to get him into college.

Rumours run rife through the sound system world. Smaller sounds, ravers, those who want to be on the inside, begin pushing for the clash of the decade. Toasters and box boys discuss and argue about the outcome. The clash reaches the pages of the *Caribbean Times* and *West Indian World* newspapers, unnamed sources giving quotes allegedly spoken by either man. One Friday, Darcus' picture appears below the 'exclusive interview' banner. He spouts on about how ungrateful Dante had become, and implies that Dante had stolen lyrics.

The scar itches. His mother's only comment is to say, "Shit!" This was probably the second time in Dante's twenty-four years that he has heard his mother swear. This public lashing hardens Dante's resolve and he continues to stretch his lyrics, his search for the right music.

He needs sex, to hold a woman, to feel his manhood appreciated. He wants to taste fresh meat and sets out that night to a new club in east London called Dougies, a club for the older, more sophisticated crowd. Perfect for finding women of a certain age, ready to be plucked without demanding too much.

He calls a minicab, despite his status as a TV-appearing-toaster and despite owning a BMW; he has not got around to getting his driving licence. Besides, the police have increased their stop and search of young black men driving cars that look better than theirs.

Dougies turns out to be a real good choice. The women outnumber the men three to one, and he was one of the younger men amongst the sea of older guys in shiny suits, over-sized rings, pork pie hats and a gold tooth that reflected the bar's lights.

Dante stands by the bar sipping a can of Brew, scanning the room until his eyes meet a woman – short, fair with a slight frame. They play eye tag until he hears the song, 'Dim the Light' by Winston Reedy. Perfect. He moves stealthily through the crowd until he is standing by her side. He touches her elbow; no words needed.

She turns, they dance, one, two, three songs. Her body feels firm and she moves like a cat, silky, languid movements that make him hard. He does not pull back and she does not pull away.

Three hours and two drinks later, he is in her bedroom. They have sex, twice, and she cooks him a nice breakfast. She does not ask when they will meet again.

By the time Dante gets home he feels strong again, and when he goes through his jacket pockets he finds a piece of paper with the woman's number and name. He looks at it for a few seconds before screwing it up and throwing it in the bin.

TONIGHT

Dante is dressed all in black and he has removed his jewellery. His scar is uncovered. He feels like a warrior dressed for battle. He smokes a spliff and says a prayer, unplanned, yet necessary. The Antonio brothers also wear black, and the Professor designs a control box that resembles the deck of a space ship. The brothers select and the Professor mixes the sound. The audience is psyched. Dante can feel Darcus' presence. Like all generals, he sent out a couple of spies, and on the night of the clash, he steps out and stands in front.

Dante and crew tease the audience, dropping rhythms, building up the tempo, slicing between Aswad, Steel Pulse, Peter Tosh and Big Youth; rough, ready Jamaican roots blended with London lovers sound Janet, Carroll, Winston, 15,16, 17... Dante's silky delivery makes the women swoon. He quotes from the Bible about Sampson and Delilah, King David and Mary Magdalene. Then he brings in Judas and the air crackles with tension, as the revellers remember their own feelings of betrayal. Dante keeps them high on the need for justice, and just before they lose control, he soothes their pain with a balm of lovers rock straight from JA in the form of John Holt and Dennis Brown.

Someone whispers that Darcus has left, and Dante smiles into the lyrics and injects some soul bounce, some two stepping. Professor and the Antonio brothers nod their heads, and Dante knows that they have won the first battle. The war is about to get bloody.

It does not take long for Darcus to win the next battle. He reveals his hand by introducing two new DJs – one sings and the other rhymes in cockney rhyming slang, a new twist. Both are fresh from the streets of London, two steps removed from the 'Windrush'.

Dante is unfazed. One thing he knows for sure: Darcus will squeeze the joy out of the two new DJs. He returns to his busy schedule of live appearances and studio time, and makes another television appearance.

Another letter from Marcia arrives, filled with descriptions of small planes, small islands, of events, carnival, and no mention of missing him. He puts her letter down.

Around the same time, his mother broaches the idea of going home to visit her sisters. It has been twenty-five years since she had walked around her mother's yard – a mother who died when she was four. She wants to take Micah to spend the summer holidays in Antigua.

Dante almost asks if he can come. He hesitates as he looks at his mum. He sees how her brief illness has aged her, yet her eyes shine brightly at the thought of going home. He nods, and offers to pay for their trip as a Mother's Day gift.

For the next couple of months, he watches as piles of clothes, suitcases, shoes and food take root from the foot of the stairs, and re-group on the landing and make a path to his mother's room.

Micah begins every sentence with, "When I go to..." Their excitement is infectious, and helps Dante set aside his feud with Darcus. Micah's mother is the only bleak spot – she tries to stop Micah from going, but is stopped by Dante's mother's implied threat of Micah's permanent removal from her life. This is enough to keep her away, this and the handful of ten pound notes Dante thrusts in her hand.

The evening before they leave, his mother, Micah and Dante sit in the kitchen as his mother once again explains who has to be paid what and when, and shows him the food in containers in the freezer. They then sit in silence. Dante can see the four locked suitcases standing in the passage, the only sign that he will be alone for six weeks. He feels nervous. It dawns on him that he has never lived alone.

Micah insists on sleeping in his room, and lies across his bed wearing one of his football t-shirts, something he often tells her not to do. He smiles.

The mini-van arrives bright and early. The driver heaves the suitcases into the back, and Dante accompanies the two loves of his heart to the airport. Another first – Micah is like a puppy on a leash, straining to run to the plane.

At the departure gate his mother faces him, smooths his leather jacket collar, and briefly touches his cheek. She says, "Not goodbye, Dante beau." She has not called him that since he was Micah's age. She hugs him quickly. Micah rushes up, kisses his cheek and squeezes his hand, then takes her grandmother's hand and looks ahead. Dante stands straining to see them as they disappear into the belly of the departure lounge.

He takes the mini-van back home, locks the front door, closes the curtains, and puts on the television and falls asleep, fully clothed on the settee. He wakes with a start, sure he hears his mother calling his name. He stretches, and hunger drives him to the kitchen, still as spotless as his mother left it. The silence of the rooms unnerves him. He puts on all the house lights, takes up the biscuit tin from the kitchen counter, makes a cup of Milo, and returns to his spot in front of the television.

He stays on the settee, dozing and watching television for the next twenty-four hours. He does not go upstairs to his bed until the sun starts peeping through the curtains, and he sleeps fitfully for a further twelve hours.

The sound of the door being pounded makes him jump out of his sleep. At first he thinks he is dreaming, until he realises that somebody is banging on his mum's front door.

He runs downstairs, slowing his movement when he sees the distinct outline of the policemen. He fixes his shirt before opening the door.

"Dante Brookes?"

"Who needs to know?"

The policemen fill the doorway, leaving no room for Dante to close the door.

"Dante Brookes?"

"Look, what you want? I know my rights, you got a search warrant?"

"Easy son. Do you know a Vince Carver of Langley Estate?"

Dante steps back and nods. Vince, his former sound brother, is in trouble and is asking for him and not Darcus.

"You need to come with us."

"Me? I ain't seen him for awhile."

"There's been an incident and he is asking to see you."

Dante recognises police speak for 'he's banged up'.

"Give me a few."

He is calm as he gets into the back of the police car, and waves at the neighbours trying to hide behind twitching curtains.

The policemen stop outside the large 'Hackney Infirmary' and he is now afraid for Vince. As they enter Casualty, Dante sees Vince's women – his mum, her face ashen and tear free, and two younger women too scared to notice that they look wild and lost. He wants to run. Too late – the three women see him. They rush towards him speaking a stream of words and sounds where only Vince's name is identifiable.

One officer tells him to stay where he is, and disappears behind a curtain. He re-appears and beckons Dante forward.

Dante glides, as he cannot hear his own feet on the hospital floor. He does not look back at the women. He goes behind the screen. Vince is a mess – bloody shirt-front, soiled trousers sliced open. The sudden smell of faeces almost makes Dante throw-up. He backs away, staring at Vince's glassy eyes and slightly opened mouth. It is the second dead body he has seen. This one, unlike Del, looks as though he can get up at any time.

"He kept asking for you, do you know why?" The officer's voice comes from somewhere far, and Dante can only shake his head.

Vince's mother clutches his arm, and he wants to pull away. Although she keeps asking why Vince wanted him, he just walks away and the officers do not stop him.

He does not attend Vince's Nine-Nights or the funeral, nor does he send a message to his mum in the West Indies.

Death on the streets is becoming a little too familiar – stabbings are ritualistic. Dante knows that not everyone is as lucky as him. He touches his scar. Darcus made it. He knows that the same man is probably making a whole show of his grief over Vince's death, and word on the street is that he paid for the funeral and played at the Nine-Nights.

Dante disappears into the studio to lay down tracks for the soon to be released film. He uses the mic to drive out his frustration, and has wordless sex with a couple of beanies who hang around the studio.

He sleeps on the settee and hardly eats in his mother's spotless kitchen. His diet consists of take-aways, biscuits and bread.

By week four, the dust is the only sign of a house unlived in. His mother's blue air mail letter arrives, filled with names of aunts and cousins who share his mother's surname. Micah sends a postcard – her tiny scrawl is crammed with delight and excitement at the sun, the goats, the cows, the hens, the mosquitoes, the bottle sodas and on and on. He smiles.

These keepsakes help him to stay present and keep his simmering anger in check. One morning, he glances at the calendar on the kitchen wall and sees that his mum and Micah's return date is two days before the film would be shown before a select audience at the Rio cinema in Dalston.

The film's director has set up some interviews with the black media, including a couple of pirate and official stations. Dante talks about his character, how he finds the film making process and the sound track. He speaks very little about himself or his family, or of anyone close to him. The questions from the female journalists centre on his looks and voice, whilst the male DJs concentrate on his lyrics and the beanies he must be meeting.

He stops reading about himself after one piece speaks of him being 'sex on legs'. He feels he has lost his edge and sounds soft.

The night before Micah and his mother return he sets about dusting and straightening cushions, as the settee sunk where his body has slept for most of the six weeks. Sleeping upstairs makes him aware of his loneliness, and the couple of nights he tries he has woken at every creak and whisper. By dawn's light he has polished and sprayed, fluffed and arranged. He gets a glimpse of himself in the hallway mirror, and see red-rimmed eyes and sallow cheeks. He has just enough time to take a cool bath and splash his face with even colder water before changing into jeans and a zip front cardigan. He grabs his wallet and keys just as the mini-van pulls up.

He hears, 'Daddy!' before he sees her. The force of her hug pushes him into a trolley, and the person tuts just as he is about to apologise. He turns back to his daughter and holds her close, inhaling her slightly sweaty scent, and then he stands back and looks at her. She is a bit taller, her skin is darker and glowing, and her hair is tightly corn rowed. She is carrying a straw basket and her wrists are encased in silver bangles.

The trolley-pusher purposefully nudges their trolley into the back of his legs, but he ignores them. He continues to ignore them until the third nudge. He turns, ready to mouth-off, but meets his mother's smiling eyes.

She looks like a younger version of the woman who left him six weeks ago, and he smiles back. He then notices that the trolley is overflowing with cases and boxes. He shakes his head.

Micah fills the mini-van with her chatter about morning breakfast, bun and cheese, malt sodas and barbeque chicken cooked on oil drums. New words mingle with her London cadence. All Dante and his mother can do is smile.

Once inside their home, his mother breathes her first words. "You clean today?"

Dante nods and she chuckles. Unpacking takes the rest of the day – gifts, letters, ground provision, sugar cakes and rum, as well as fried fish wrapped in foil and burnt carvings of the coat of arms.

It strikes Dante that his mum's island is a real place with its own flag, coat of arms, shops and language. It is like discovering that Jack really did discover another land at the top of the beanstalk.

Micah talks until her head suddenly drops sideways. Dante carries her to her room, but when he returns from his late night session, he finds her asleep across his bed with one of his football shirts under her head. He shakes his head and places a blanket and pillow on the floor, and sleeps soundly.

CLASH

Dante's invitation to the film's preview, titled 'Clash', lay on the kitchen table where his mother fills the space with smoke and frying hair and oil. His mum does not believe in chemicals, however, she has no problem hot combing her hair for special occasions. Usually Micah would ask to have her hair done, however, right now she is still in love with her corn rows.

Dante has purchased a new suit from a tailor who is an apprentice on Savile Row. It is made from soft cashmere wool and it fits him like a glove. He wears a silk shirt, no tie and the softest kid leather shoes. By the time he manages to get his mother and daughter into the film-sponsored car, he is feeling like he has drunk three Brews and smoked too much weed. Not even his mother's prayer for a safe passage calms him.

He is sure that his mother can hear his heart beating through his shirt. He is not expecting anything special as they pull up outside of the Rio cinema, until he steps out of the car and he hears a pop and sees a flash. He feels himself hunch down as he puts his arm out to stop his mother walking in front of him. It takes him a few moments for him to realise what Micah is saying: "Cameras, you must be famous," and he laughs. His mother and Micah flank him either side, and he is sure their smiles are wider than his. He hears his name and he nods in recognition. When they reach the entrance, a woman in black separates him from his two women and he watches as they are escorted behind the double doors.

He waits, and feels his cheeks ache as he sucks them in to stop himself from smiling too hard; that cheesy, "Mum, I'm on TV" grin. Another woman steps forward, and he notices her sparkling green eye-shadow. It is the director's assistant. He walks towards her and they are ushered through a side door. The lights are dimmed and an MC introduces the actors, writer and director, one by one. Dante is told to walk towards the light, and a man with a microphone shoves it in his face and asks him how he felt about the preview.

"Blessed," he whispers.

He thinks he hears "Daddy" and waves towards the voice. He joins the director and the other guests in the front row.

The lights go down and the audience goes quiet. Dante's side profile fills the screen. His face is peering into a shoe shop window, admiring the high-polished Italian shoes. The camera pulls back and he is standing next to a shopping cart, and two older women are next to him holding court about Sunday church. The audience laughs and Dante relaxes, sinks down in his chair, watches and listens...

People clap, whistle, sing-a-long, whisper, laugh, some even sniff.

"What do you hope to achieve with this movie?"

"Is it a true representation of life for young black youth?"

"Did you know Dante could act?"

"Do you want to make more films?"

The questions and answers come thick and fast.

The car ride home is quiet as Micah sleeps and his mother also closes her eyes. Once he puts Micah to bed, he comes downstairs to watch late night television, a mix of education programmes and dull dramas. He is so lost in his thoughts that he does not hear his mother enter the room until she touches the top of his head. The touch is so light that he is not sure if she kissed or touched him. He did, however, hear her say, "I am so proud of you, Dante. I love you." But she turns, leaving the room before he can acknowledge her presence.

He carries this warm feeling around for a while, pulling it out whenever he feels he needs to give Babylon a good arse kicking – such as whenever a policeman looks at him or drives slowly past as he carries a bag of sweets for Micah. Or when young, white males eyed him up with faces filled with promise and betrayed by bodies tight with fear. This feeling gives him courage to stand firm, yet Darcus remains in the shadows, reminding him that real men need more than their mother's love.

Dante goes back to work in the clubs, the blues dances, his familiar haunts. More beanies approach him; most ignore him. Yet, when he is on the mic, he speaks directly to them and wears down their defences until he is their defender, speaking their truths.

And for all of this, just before he closes his eyes he can hear Del and Vince urging him to deal with Darcus – deal with him.

He calls a meeting with the Professor and the Antonio brothers – it is time.

Professor is the one who comes up with the how. Simple – it will take place where all soundmen got their start – a youth club, a back in the day, a pound a head. They will go lyric for lyric, the audience deciding the winner, 'the King of the Sounds' – reputation the ultimate reward.

Dante speaks to his producer, and he loves the idea of a 'live' set being sold as an LP. The producer approaches Darcus, and as Dante had predicted, Darcus haggles for a very good percentage of the sales.

Dante shrugs at the financial demands – he has many warriors to defend. Tickets are not going to be sold, it is going to be first come, first served. On the night, the line stretches along the high street. Bouncers are hired to ensure that no knifeman will take away the limelight. The best looking and the best dressed girls are let in, followed by men in suits, trench coats and the occasional dread. This was the clash of the pretty London boys, not for the hardcore reggae fans who had natty dreads, smoked unfiltered weed and 'reason', to the lyrics of Peter Tosh, Black Uhuru and the like.

The set-up took two days. The hall is taken over by the Professor, and Darcus' new engineer, Bill. Neither man speaks as they set up in their respective sides of the hall. None of the DJs practiced there – they will be unveiled tonight.

Dante and the Antonio brothers are ushered through the back entrance. The heat and the smoke welcomes them. Dante feels thirteen – the age he was when he first heard a sound in action. Those guys were five years older, and played dub plates and reggae tunes imported from Jamaica. They wore dark clothes and big hats stuffed with hair. Youths like Dante wanted to be them, to smoke as hard as them and copy their speech, idiom for idiom. Now Dante is the one being copied.

Tonight he is wearing black, plus a large, gold cross and chain. The Professor and the Antonio brothers are also wearing black – Adidas tracksuits with the distinctive white stripes down the side of the pants and jacket.

Professor warms the set with a specially recorded dub slate, and heads are bobbing. Professor and Darcus tossed a coin and Darcus will play first. Dante knows that he will play snatches of sounds to test the crowd, to tease Dante in the hope that he will reveal his special tunes first.

The rhythms change thick and fast. The ravers show their appreciation by sounding off, singing along, and the DJs rewind the tracks and fill the air with special effects, echoes, whistles and horns.

True to form, Darcus' challenge increases in tempo until he reveals his hand, a young vocalist whose looks make up for his limited voice range. He charms the ladies, and Dante smiles and nods to the Professor just as the young pretender runs out of steam. The Antonio brothers unleash a dub track with a catchy back beat that makes the ravers nod, and the tempo shifts as Dante begins his sermon. He draws on their common church upbringing, their black conscious awakening, and ends with a call to arm themselves with knowledge.

Darcus' DJ shoots back with a call to burn down Babylon and the air is now thick, and the young men feel for their missing blades. Dante steps in and pours down lyrics of blessings leading to love – men pull women to dance, rough grinds become tender two steps, women and men sing to each other. Although Darcus' DJ sings about brown eyed girls and simple kisses, Dante stays ahead as he whispers sex and dimmed lights, a space where they can forget about the world outside.

Professor and the Antonio brothers blend tracks, sound effects, back beats and old beats seamlessly with total control, and Dante is the wordsmith and circus ringmaster directing and changing the tempo at will. Yet, he keeps his ears tuned to hear Darcus' ace. He feels the tempo shift slightly before he hears it. It is a sound based on the streets of London – no hint of the original Jamaican mento/ska beats – this is a simple, soulful, easy on the ear sound and encourages the ravers to dance.

For three tracks Darcus runs the dance, and Dante is impressed as it is an original move, almost. In the middle of the fourth track, the smooth lyrics of the young singer are beginning to sound familiar, and he makes one simple mistake: he repeats a phrase. In the semi-darkness, Dante feels the Antonio brothers smile. The war is coming to an end, real soon. Darcus is about to feel the full force of Dante's rage – legal murder. He will cut Darcus note by note, lyric by lyric. He bows his head, reveals his scar, and he hears Del say, "Now." He places the mic before his lips and chants the 23rd Psalm.

"The Lord is my shepherd; I shall not want. He maketh me to lie down in green pastures; He leadeth me beside the still waters..."

And the ravers stand still, caught out by the intensity of his delivery. The beat changes and falls like rain drops on hot asphalt. Each sizzle is deep-rooted in his need to make Darcus pay, his father pay, Sheila pay, and Del also had to pay, for having left him.

The chant increases, his voice fluid and strong. Each word nicks like tiny paper cuts. By the time the ravers whistle and ask for a rewind Dante could no longer see – the word 'bloodclart' uttered by Darcus' DJ signals the end.

The Antonio brothers unleash the sound of London soul – happy sounds and the ravers get dancing. Dante rests his voice, and the Antonio brothers use the mic to tease the beanies that smile at them and encourage the men to hold onto their woman.

They almost miss the sound of skin being slapped – it happens just as the ravers are about to two-step like their parents. A scream and a sound made Dante's scar burn. Ravers charge for the exit and bouncers are moved like pebbles skimming the water's surface.

The Antonio brothers and Professor push Dante down, covering his body, and pull him towards the back entrance. By the time the police arrive and cordon off the roadside most of the ravers have disappeared, leaving behind the DJs, bouncers and some passers-by.

Dante and his crew are sitting on the pavement as the ambulance crew wheel out two stretchers with blood soaked white sheets, yet both faces are uncovered. One appears to be crying and the other is mumbling.

Dante stands up and he locks eyes with Darcus, the mumbling man on the second stretcher. Neither man stops looking at each other, right up until they close the ambulance door.

Dante, the Professor and the Antonio brothers make their way to Professor's flat, and smoke weed and drink beers to dull the fear knifing through them. One of the Antonio brothers tries to explain what he heard happen in Darcus' corner – it is the youth with the good looks who felt that Darcus had dissed him, and this youth sliced Darcus before the last beat. Then someone else sliced the youth and the blood spurted. Men and women ran and police question many, yet nobody saw.

They fall asleep, each fighting dreams of dying on cold pavements with policemen peering at their bodies and joking about, "One down, a few more to go," while their mothers' tears drop onto their blood-soaked bodies. Dante thinks he hears his mother scream. His eyes burn and he needs air and water. His head throbs; it feels too heavy, too full. This feeling frightens him. It is a feeling of nothing, of being responsible for the bloodshed. He feels the bile in his throat and just makes it to a sink before it all comes out. None of the others move and they appear to be suffering just as much – their eyes dart about behind stretched eyelids.

Dante cleans the sink and splashes his face with cold water. He tries to light another spliff and the smell repulses him.

He puts on the radio. A pirate station is playing Dante's tracks, and the excitable announcer speaks of blood on the dance floor, a clash to end all clashes, and declares Dante the winner. He adds that the injured men are in hospital recovering and that it is best Darcus stays there, as he is done. He switches off the radio and lets out a loud chewpts.

Later that day he goes home and finds his daughter sitting wide eyed at the kitchen table. Dante's very agitated mother explains that the police visited his home. The police made her think he was dead. The police have now darkened her door twice, and both times involved stabbing and Darcus.

She asks Dante if he thinks God is sleeping, and she proceeds to pray, quietly at first. But then the fear takes over, and it all comes tumbling out mixed with Psalms beseeching God's help. She prays until her tears become Dante's and his knees feel the cold linoleum floor. Micah whispers, "Amen."

GROWING PAINS

His mother takes telephone calls from his producer; he just wants peace. His mother cooks for him, yet leaves him alone. She walks around him, and Micah does not sleep in his room.

He does not smoke weed, or feel the need to smoke any weed. Nor does he visit Del; he just wants to stay home. He writes words that go from single sentences to paragraphs, to a story which starts with a boy waiting for his father to come home.

He has bought a colour television for his bedroom, and is flicking between a program on the life of bees and a children's puppet show when Micah knocks. She pushes the door open and in her hand is a thin, blue airmail letter. She places the letter on his lap while glancing at the television, and disappears.

The letter lay there unopened for a good hour or two, until he learnt that the queen bee uses her drones until they die. He smiles, trying to imagine what woman could do that to him. Would he even let a woman do that to him? Right now, Marcia's letters make him feel like he is travelling with her. He opens her letter carefully, smooths the pages and reads it line by line. He smells the fruits ripening on the trees and hears the noisy bus horns. She ends with "it's time for me to come back, are you going to meet me at the airport?"

He did not expect her to ask, and in that moment he knows that she is the side of him he needs to make him whole. He places the letter on his Bible and wonders if he could have a normal life, maybe settle with Marcia and they all live together. Would he continue as a soundman, or would he get a job in the Post Office or at British Telecom? He chuckles. Retiring from the club scene at the ripe old age of twenty-five? What would Del say?

He checks the letter again and sees that Marcia's return date is the 10th. He checks the newspaper and sees that it is the 8th. He looks in the mirror, and sees an older man with straggly beard and an uneven afro. His eyes are flat, too little sleep and not enough weed. He decides to visit the one person who will let him talk about Marcia without feeling weak... Del, his bredren and blood. He grabs a handful of cash and his keys, then digs around in his wardrobe until he finds a small foil packet. He sniffs the contents, still fresh and strong. He then pops his head round the living room door and says, "Just going down the road," and he is out.

He stops at the off-license, buys two cans of Brew and a packet of ten Benson & Hedges cigarettes.

The churchyard is empty and slightly damp despite the promise of sunshine. Del's headstone is clean except for a few flowers. Dante touches them before he sits down and slowly builds a spliff. He licks the edges of the Rizla paper, sprinkling the herb and a few seeds and then rolls the paper between his fingers. He lights it, inhales deeply and blows the smoke through his nose and over the headstone. The act serves as a cleaning, a libation, a greeting. He sits still and listens for Del's voice. When the sound of rushing wind fills his ears, he nods.

He feels Del sit down next to him and they calmly inhale from the spliff. Del smiles, and his teeth are still even and white. At first his voice is muffled, distant, until Dante draws closer. Del's words float like music. "'D', you is still a man?" and, "Don't let them run you." Another drag, another exhale. Del's features are stretched and almost transparent. Dante giggles and Del suddenly gets up and starts walking away. Dante tries to hail his friend, to make him turn around and reason some more. However, as Del moves behind the church wall, Dante feels good; no tears, just good.

By the time he leaves the cemetery and walks towards the barbers, it is turning dark. He has been talking to Del for over four hours. Luckily, the barbers is still open, filled with guys discussing the weekend football matches, beanies and raves. The radio accompanies their conversation, alternating between lovers rock and new, London soul. Dante nods his acknowledgement, takes his place on the long bench and leafs through a newspaper.

The buzzing of the shears, the warmth of the paraffin heater and the droning of the radio lulls him to sleep. It was wordless, dreamless, and the barber's light touch on his shoulder shocks him awake. He thinks he sees his father looking back at him. He blinks and sees himself, trimmed, neat and slightly older than the youth who toasted on the Rodigan show. He pays the barber and walks home.

Dinner is silent, very silent, and yet, comfortable. He books a minicab for the early morning and goes to bed.

The airport at 6.30 in the morning is incredibly quiet, apart from a mechanical voice that squeaks over an antenna, and rubber on lino. Dante tries to work out if he is at the right terminal, and sees that he has twenty minutes to find it before her flight arrives.

He watches as people emerge from behind double doors, blinking at the terminal's unnatural brightness as they try to push unwieldy trolleys packed with cases and boxes. He sucks a mint, rolls it around with his tongue and almost misses her, having bitten his inner cheek and closed his eyes. When he opens them there she is, standing in front of him. She is bronzed, healthy and glowing.

They hug, and then he looks at her again and they hug some more, both grinning like the chimpanzees in the tea advert on television. He pushes her trolley and asks her to come home with him – she hesitates before stopping at a phone booth. Her call is brief and she agrees to spend the weekend with him. They eat breakfast with his mum and Micah. He runs her a hot bath and washes her back, and as she dozes off he wraps her up and lies beside her on his bed.

Dante feels a peace, an ease of spirit he has not felt before. He has no frame of reference for this feeling. It has come close a few times, but this time the feeling stays, even as she sleeps without them having sex and he holds her hand.

The days roll on: breakfast, writing, sleep, television, dinner, studio, breakfast. His album is taking shape, and the music speaks of London nights, easy lyrics and light rhythms. Dante wants to give the ravers a nice time – to dance, to sing, to be totally free.

There is an unspoken chapter between Dante and Marcia. he wants to know why she left, and yet, he drifts into the feeling as Marcia is there, always there, openly loving him, sometimes with sex, sometimes with a touch and sometimes with questions as well as she listened. Her stillness makes him speak. And one night, he tells her about Del – his last visit, and his continued visits to the cemetery. She holds him while he speaks, and for the second time in his adult life he cries in front of a woman who was not his mother. No sound, just tears, rivers of tears. Tears that cleansed his pain.

The next morning they make love, slowly and with an intensity they have never shared before, both with their eyes wide open. He knew just then that he wanted Marcia to stay with him.

This feeling makes him smile, even as he walks to the barber's. He is blissfully unaware of being watched. He goes into the barbers and takes a seat, nods at his barber and picks up a newspaper.

He hears Darcus just before he realises that he is standing in front of him. Dante puts down the newspaper. Darcus is dishevelled, red-eyed and slightly unsteady.

"You couldn't make it without me. I made you. Me, you understand? Me. I gave you money for your weed and the music, you is still a bwoy, just a bwoy."

Dante does not move. He just keeps looking at the man standing in front of him with an ugly scar running from below his right eye to the tip of his chin. His eyes are red and watery. He keeps speaking, rambling. However, he does not move any closer to Dante.

The barbers gather silently in a semi-circle behind Darcus, scissors in view. No customers move. Darcus opens his mouth again and Dante punches him in the stomach. Darcus doubles over and hisses as the air escapes his opened mouth and replaces any words he has lined up to spew all over Dante. Dante raises his foot and steps over him, and walks out of the barbers to the sound of clapping and thuds.

He is not sure where he should go and just keeps walking, accompanied by the vision of Darcus' ugly scar and mad look. He feels as ugly as Darcus, a man no longer so powerful, trying to be big. Dante runs his fingers across the scar across his neck; is this how it would end for all of them? He shudders ... what was it that they were all fighting so hard to hold onto? Who really cares if they are big men? The knife makes talking redundant, and a scar is a sign that you have survived a moment – not a war.

He walks until his feet hurt, and finds that he is in front of his primary school gates. He watches the youngsters as they charge about playing the games he played – 'bulldog', 'tag' and 'kiss chase'. He smiles; life was so bloody simple back then. The colour of his skin meant little to him. His best friend was a boy from Cyprus, Mario, and they shared a common love for puppet shows and DC comics. It has been years since Dante thought about Mario. They had lost touch once they went to secondary school, and now Dante wonders if Mario became a comic book artist. What had he wanted to be? He dug deep, past the memories of hours spent in youth clubs with his guys listening to sound systems, and his father being in the house, to his love of story time, and going to the library and reading books in the stuffy, quiet, wooden room. He loved the smell of the musty books and would disappear, seeing the fields, hearing the pirates, and never questioning that none of the characters looked like him.

It is only now, older and more aware of how his colour separated him in the classrooms and on the streets, that he used the mic as his weapon of choice. He looks at the old, brick building with wide windows, much smaller now, and yet, he had felt safe. Now there is so much blood and loss. He has more money than he ever thought he could earn, a woman who keeps him reaching inward and loves him, a daughter who worships his every move, and the burden of betrayal by people close to him with a scar as a constant reminder.

As Dante walks away, he realises that he has no plans, no vision of himself as an older man. It has all been about the music, the vibe, the weed, the lyrics; his fame feels accidental. And now he is tired of having to fight off Darcus' long shadow.

He needs weed, he needs Marcia, and he needs to stop thinking so much. It will turn him crazy, or so his mother said once as he sat staring into space.

The evening turns cool, and he pulls up his collar and tries to warm his fingers in his jeans pockets. Dante walks and ignores the people around him and the warm glow of the street lights. He is sure people can hear him thinking. They dodge him as he walks with purpose towards the park.

He sits on the roundabout until the park keeper shouts, "It's time to lock the gates!" For the first time in his life he does not want to go home. He wishes for a place of his own, somewhere he could write all night and sleep when it turns dawn without explaining to anyone.

He finally goes home after stopping to buy some chips and a piece of cod doused in salt and vinegar. When he sits down in his mother's clean and quiet kitchen he knows that he would miss this, this connection; his feet are rooted in this house. He is where he needs to be.

In the morning, his mother makes him oats porridge spiced with nutmeg and honey. He eats quietly and tries to imagine Marcia in their kitchen. He cannot see her doing this. She has shown no interest in cooking on a daily basis.

The next few weeks are spent in the studio working with a new lovers rock singer, a guy with a silky voice and twisted locks. They do not speak much as he always has a beanie with him. Dante is sure that two of them are pregnant, but he does not ask, nor did he comment. Dante listens to the singer's tracks; they are more commercial than he is used to, and yet it is flying off the shelves in both pop and reggae record stores. He starts toasting over them. Three days into the recording session he starts to shorten the phrases, keeping them tight and playful. The singer tries once or twice to suggest changes, however, Dante ignores him and presses on.

His next date is a sportswear party at a club. He buys a new tracksuit and pairs it with a white vest and a pair of Adidas trainers. He is taking Marcia with him – their first official outing as girlfriend and boyfriend. The beanies will now know that he is no longer on the market. She chose a netball skirt and tracksuit top in white. She will look fresh and classy.

SPORTS COCKTAIL

The sound scene is taking a new direction – most toasters were now DJs, more interested in having a good time and playing songs that make the ravers feel good than speaking of the streets. The clothes are of a finer quality; leather softer and suits cleaner and leaner. The women are becoming sexier, with backless evening dresses, and high-heeled shoes that are strappy and expose painted toes. Dante loves seeing their toes, and encourages Marcia to buy a pair, which she wears once and bitches about the whole night.

Dante's tunes are still being played on the radio stations, both pirate and mainstream, and one day a magazine asks him to write about the reggae scene. He laughs. It is Marcia who stands in front of him and says, "Dante you can do this... write what you know, and you know this."

It takes him five days before he knows where to start – Papa Sam's, where all sound men get their rhythms, their history lesson and, once in a blue moon, a little Jamaican white rum.

Dante and Papa Sam chat for two hours, in between listening to scratchy seven-inchers and looking at black and white images of Papa Sam when he "first come ah Britain" – young and ambitious, working in factories and going to house parties, going home to Jamaica and bringing back fresh recordings, and doing this for too many years to mention.

Dante writes an article in long hand. He asks Marcia to look it over, and she offers to type it for him. He feigns indifference, yet is secretly pleased when she says, "It is a good, honest piece." His CSE English grade 1 is not wasted.

The article appears with his picture and name at the bottom. 'School for Reggae' by Dante Brooks. And yes, his mother cuts it out and keeps it. The magazine asks him to write other articles, the next being a chat with one of his reggae heroes, Gregory Isaacs. He has four weeks to produce it. The evening with Gregory Isaacs and his band is a mix of reasoning, toasting, singing and smoking.

Marcia offers to teach him to type and buys him a small, yet modern, portable typewriter. They practice until he stops sulking about the slowness of the keys and the letters not being in a straight line. He starts practicing late at night, until his mother stops him. Then he tries whilst Micah is around, and she soon takes over. His interview with Gregory takes five days and many sheets of paper to type, and again the editor liked it. Marcia jokes that had she known that she could have become a writer by being a soundman first, she would have skipped college. He has the good grace to take it as a compliment.

The hours he spends writing take him away from his preparation for the sports dance, and he finds that he does not want to go. It no longer holds power over him. His lyrics are getting stronger and longer – they are telling stories and have meaning.

The noise, the smoke, the murmuring, and the constant need to be 'hard' and always in control, is making him tired. He wants out, yet there is nothing else he can do; he does not want to be a British Telecom engineer or a post office worker. Although, the thought of driving a big red bus does make him smile. His father was a bus driver, and he used to travel with him sometimes, sitting in the seat behind the driver's cab. Every time he brought the bus to a bus stop, Dante's father would look back and smile at him. The memory jolts him and he writes it down. If he could draw, he would have sketched his father's face. The moment passes as fleetingly as a wisp of ganja smoke, and yet, like the scent of herb, that vision clings to him.

On the night of the sports dance Marcia is tense and distant, and every interaction feels as though they are on the verge of fighting. Dante cannot figure out what is making her act like this. Is it something he had done, not done, said, or not said? He lets it slide and concentrates on the set. Everyone at the dance looks like an older version of their school self – tracksuits, football and netball kits, a few tennis outfits and even a cricketer complete with pads and cap. The air is happy, and simple rhythms cover the room with joy. No one is thinking about the world beyond this dance.

Dante's lyrics reflect his maturity and inner search. The crowd sings along and smiles. At first Dante thinks that they are laughing at him, and he feels his inner core recoil, until he realises that these ravers are not afraid to show that they are happy. He laughs, and the Professor mixes this sound into the opening of a chirpy little number by the recently deceased Bob Marley.

By morning the pristine sportswear looks a little more raggedy, and eyes open wide in the morning sun.

Dante takes Marcia to a local bagel shop for a little breakfast of smoked salmon and cream cheese. She takes one bite and gags. Dante recognises that look of fear in her eyes; it is the look Sheila had when she told him about her pregnancy. He wants to dance and chant and smoke and laugh. Then he sees that Marcia is not as happy. He wants to ask, but her body says, "No."

They travel home in silence, and it is not until they are in his bedroom that she says, "I am pregnant." Then the tears fall, and her shoulders heave up and down.

She does not want his child.

The thought winds him and he drops on his bed. He has no words, and the irony makes him chuckle. She stands, he sits, and they do not look at each other.

Finally, he asks, "Why don't you want my baby?"

She steps back. "I do want your baby, but not now, we are not ready for this. I am not ready for this. We do not have a home of our own. I am about to start work at a new television station and you are..."

"Just a DJ, a sound man."

"You are not listening Dante. I love you, and this is not right for..."

"You."

"No, us."

He puts up his hand and she stops talking. He wants to shout, but he does not want to wake his mother or Micah. He stays sitting on the bed as Marcia steps towards him and kneels down before him. She does not touch him.

"Dante, we do not need this baby right now. We need to be in a position to be on our own. We have not lived together. You don't know that I usually only have coffee for breakfast, and that I like to read in the evenings when I am not trying to write. Do you know that I like listening to the radio more than watching television? I know *your* routine, I know *your* loves, and yet, you don't know..."

"I know I love you, and is that not enough?"

Finally, Marcia touches him. He fights the urge to hurt her, yet he wants her to hold him.

There are no tears, and a voice from within tells him to move away. He stands up and tries to control his breathing. She starts to follow him.

He needs space, he needs room to think.

He hears her talking about their age and the future and he wants to slap her, he wants to scream at her. He shrugs his shoulders and turns towards her. She steps back as though she is afraid of him.

"You don't care?"

He does not answer, as he is scared that his voice is not strong enough. He looks away.

He hears the door closing, and the soft click allows him to exhale. He goes to bed, still dressed, and sleeps. When he wakes up, it is dark.

She does not want his baby. She does not want his baby. The words grow louder and louder in his head. He starts to thump his pillow until it is shapeless. How could she not want his child? He has money. His mother would help, and Micah is old enough to help as well.

He tries to reason, but his mind will not free up.

He stays in his room, fighting with the words that echo through him and touch memories he does not want to examine. He feels a pain deep inside, and he doubles over and clutches his sheets.

Dante does not speak to Marcia for a couple of days, and she stays away until the third day, when she calls. He answers and agrees to meet at the burger bar he took her to after their first cinema date. They sit in a booth with a plate of chips between them. Dante sips on a tasteless fizzy drink and Marcia stirs a muddy cup of coffee.

Marcia speaks first, her voice firm, yet low. "I have thought this through, trust me. I have made an appointment with a clinic and want you to know that I am going to go through with this. I..."

Dante opens his mouth, but Marcia touches his arm. This silences him. "Dante, I do want your baby, just not now. I need you to understand this."

Dante looks at her, and for the first time he is really hearing her, and yet he wants to be the one making the decision. He has a child and he knows the fear he felt when he saw Micah for the first time. He never saw that fear in Sheila's eyes, and now Micah is living with him and does not ask for her mother, calling his mother "Mama".

The light is harsh and shows the dark circles under her eyes. He is not sure what to say – the man in him wants this baby, but the part of him that is awakening to Marcia understands.

The answer comes to him in a form of a question – does he want Marcia to leave his life? His sigh is the only answer Marcia receives.

Three days later, he is holding her hand in a grey room filled with posters about contraception, and dog-eared magazines. The rest of the room is filled with women, some young with grim faced mothers and others not so young, dressed well and twiddling with jewellery. He is the only man, and all of them look at him. He feels like he is being cussed, as he represents why they are all there. Marcia squeezes his hand and he sits up. No words pass between them until they are lying on his bed later. Marcia is weeping silently, and Dante tries not to think about the child he wanted and she did not.

They do not speak about the abortion.

It is his mother who raised the idea of "what next?" for that nice girl and him. Dante smiles and kisses her on the cheek; she does not say anymore. He takes Micah to the park, and realises that she is too big for the kids' section. When did this happen? She is animated, talking about 'Miriam' and 'Wendy' and some boy called 'Titus'. Dante tries to keep up with the changing loyalties and arguments, and ends up smiling. After several swing sessions and endless "watch me daddy" as she slides down the 'big' slide, she stands before him slightly flushed with hands on hips. "Daddy, when are you going to marry Marcia? She's really nice."

Dante starts laughing. "Did granny tell you to ask me this?"

She shakes her head. "No, silly, she's just so nice. She's pretty and she likes to read to me, and she tried to help granny in the kitchen."

"And what does Granny say?"

"She says she's a nice girl, and that you should marry her before someone else does."

"You have plenty of chat for a little girl, maybe you too big for an ice cream?"

"Daddy, I am never too big for ice cream."

He hugs her, inhaling her strawberry scent, and they head towards the ice cream van.

Micah's question and simple statements slowly get under Dante's skin, though he tries to ignore them. He's sharp and antsy. He tries to write a composition, which he then turns into lyrics for a new track he is supposed to record with a new DJ, who is combining soul tracks with DJ lyrics, a whole new London sound.

The recording session takes place in north London, in an area he was not used to. They move differently, and dress like art students. However, their singing is almost church like, and Dante finds that he has to measure his tone and delivery to match theirs. The match-up is seamless, and the DJ asks him to write some lyrics for him and they will pay him for them separately.

Dante takes the tube home and marvels at the different twists and turns his life is taking, from Marcia to writing. He does not feel any different, and according to his reflection does not look any different, yet there is stuff in his mind that will not let him settle. Up to now he thought his life was pretty complete, and now he is thinking about fitting one woman into his life. Was he really thinking about marriage? He has never lived with a woman. Well, not in his own place. He has very rarely stayed over at Marcia's place – her bedsit – as she mainly comes to him; it is just easier to go to his home.

The rocking of the tube train makes him doze, and only instinct wakes him just as it pulls into his station. It is busy and noisy and filled with youths with hard faces, too young to be so angry. Some recognise him and nod their acknowledgement. As he moves along the high street, his mind turns to Del, his one true friend, who left him. He knows a lot of people, and occasionally he hangs out with Professor and the Antonio brothers and they reason about music and life as black men in Babylon. And yet, he does not know about their families. Darcus' betrayal has ensured that he stays outside of other men's lives.

He finds himself in front of the café, where back in the day the four of them would eat greasy, full English breakfasts and drink dark, strong tea. He looks in the window and sees four young black men laughing and eating. He debates whether he should go in, and decides that he would be better off moving forward. He decides to go the bagel bar around the corner, and buys a bagel with salmon and cream cheese and a strong black coffee.

He stands in front of St Mark's church. Its gates are wide open and, unusually, so is its door. He swallows the last of his bagel and walks into the church building. It is cool and dark, slightly musty, and there are shadows sitting in pews. He sits down and listens to the mumbling and his own heart beat. He has no idea how long he sits there. Inner words untangle from jumble to a single line: "Be a man, Dante." He shakes his head, but the line refuses to go away. He wants to ask what he means. He *is* a man, he loves like a man, he earns his own money and he has a daughter. His mind turns to the child, the one that Marcia said they did not need right now, and his fist clenches. Had he been a man when he said nothing about the pain this is causing him, or how he dreams of holding another baby, a son?

The dark, cool interior comforts him, and the shadows pass without intruding on his space. The urge to light a spliff right there in the pew grows strong, and he feels around in his pockets. Nothing. He realises that he has not smoked any weed for weeks, or drunk much Brew.

Eventually, by the time he leaves, his thoughts are no longer just about him; stuff is being stripped away. He is starting to make decisions that no longer centre on him. He is so engrossed in his happy thoughts that he does not see the man standing by the gate until he calls his name.

I AM A MAN

Dante looks at the man with the head of hair sprouting from beneath a floppy hat. His eyes look familiar, yet the rest of his face is covered in hair, like his beard begins at his eyebrows. He is smiling, or appears to be smiling, although Dante is not sure as his deep yellow teeth make a line through his beard.

Dante keeps moving, and the man touches his arm. Dante stands off, ready to throw a punch. The man does not flinch and begins instead to quote scriptures. "Honour thy mother and thy father so that thy days may be long."

His voice pulls a memory from his youth; it had said, "Just going down the road." He stares at the bushman before him and says nothing, although he keeps his distance and slows his breathing.

The man senses his unease and mirrors Dante's stance. They face off like gunslingers in a bad western.

Finally, the man speaks. "Dante, you grow into a fine man, and just like me you love the music. I used to follow you from dance to dance and listen to you chat pon de mic and you strong, real strong."

Dante does not answer. He shrugs his shoulders and stares at the man.

"Your mother do a good job of turning you against me..."

"You left us for a pack of fags."

"You was too young to remember how it was for your mother and me, you don't know..."

"I was there, remember, I was always there."

"You don't know nothing; how that woman would make me feel bad, or how I watch her fill your head with rubbish about me and my family."

Dante opens his mouth to speak when he realises that the man is standing still, mouth opening and closing but with no words. The man begins to dance, a Rasta man two step. The conversation is over, and when Dante whispers, "Dad," the man continues his dance and even appears to smile at someone other than Dante.

Dante moves away from the man, his eyes stinging. This man could not be his father. This time the memory drawer in his heart is shut tight, with a big red sign: 'Toxic'. He wipes his hand across his eyes; he would shed no tears. That man is now dead.

By the time he gets home he feels oddly lighter, as though something important has happened. For the first time in a long time, Dante feels free. He runs up to his room and begins writing. The urge to fill pages with words is strong, but his pen is not strong enough. He grabs his typewriter and begins striking the keys. His typing is relentless, pounding the letters onto the page. Words are jumbled, with no punctuation. Punching the keys drags out all the self pity.

He feels someone touching his shoulder, and he draws back his fist until he hears Marcia's voice. He has fallen asleep on the desk, and scattered around his feet are sheets of paper filled with words. He blinks and stretches while Marcia picks up the papers. He can see that she is wary, and careful not to get too close to him.

He needs to hold her, yet he is still trying to understand why he wants to hit her, hurt her. They have been dancing around each other for weeks, and his mother has commented that something is not right with them.

She speaks softly, yet her body is rigid and her eyes are flat. "Your mum called me, worried about your all-night typing. Are you ok?"

His "No" pushes her closer to the door and roots him to his chair. All the words stored inside him are now laid bare on sheets of white paper. He has nothing left to say.

She places the stack of papers on the bed and leaves the room. Questions and tears hang between them, and they are both too tired to reach out.

Dante gets up, pushes the papers on the floor and falls on the bed. He sleeps for hours. He wants to dream of better times with Del, and Marcia, the girl with the lovely smile.

Three days later he emerges fresh faced and clear eyed. He has placed Marcia in a draw next to Del; he could not be with her anymore.

The producer from north London calls, making Dante an offer to travel with his crew across the UK – a tour, like a pop band. They would be playing to all kinds of people, no longer just black clubs and blues dances. Six weeks, twelve shows, and he would earn as much as he did in a year of dances.

Micah is excited and pleads to come on the tour. She is denied twice, by Dante and his mother.

As he packs he finds a small, ladies t-shirt. It smells of Marcia, and he places it among his clothes.

On stage, he personifies London coolness – fine clothes, 'criss' hair cut, trim beard, and chat that charmed the beanies from in front of the stage to his bed. Black, white, half-caste, he does not care. They service him, and he makes sure they leave before breakfast.

By week five, all the beanies look the same. A few have travelled from city to city to be with him, though he doesn't care to be with them for longer than the sex lasts.

In the mornings, he smokes two cigarettes and tries to write.

It is the producer, the group leader, who puts him straight. "You are not a man 'cause you sleep with plenty women; you is a man 'cause you know what you want and you know how Jehovah created you."

Dante stops sleeping with the beanies, and instead reasons with the producer into the early hours of the morning. During one early morning talking session, just as the producer starts to rise, Dante lets it out. All the fears, the sorrow, the lost child, his love, his loathing, his need for Marcia. He talks until his eyes burn and his mouth becomes dry.

The last man he spoke to like this was Del, as he lay in the grounds of St Mark's cemetery. His own need to speak frightens him, and yet he cannot not stop the train of words and thoughts.

The producer does not interrupt him. When he runs out of words, the two men sit in silence.

In that silence Dante feels his body tingling.

"You is a real man Dante, your feelings are yours. Go find your queen and tell her what you feel. She hurt too. Whatever you think you know, you feel differently. It's time to stop running, stand on your ground and speak. Now, rest up. We have one more show to do and we going to end big."

Dante sleeps like a man at peace, and he wakes with new words at his fingertips.

That night the crowd's energy fills them makes them high with it. Dante's words and the music hit a sweet spot. Everyone is smiling, even after Dante releases 'Baby Father', his take on the joys and pain of being a young father. If the group is taken by surprise they do not show it, and they let him ride his rhythm.

They head to London, and they chat and buzz until the sun comes up. As they drop him off outside his home, the producer says, "You is a star, Dante, we gonna reach well beyond these shores."

They touch fists to seal the deal.

He hears his mother singing and he walks into the kitchen – she stops singing long enough to say that he looks hungry. He laughs and they hug briefly.

"Go wash up and come down for some breakfast. Put your washing by the machine."

His mother's new pride and joy – a top-loading washing machine – stands gleaming in the corner. It still had its protective plastic cover over the controls.

Dante is too tired to do more than she asks. His room is small and dark and filled with his man self – his clothes are hung on the wardrobe door, his chest of drawers can barely close. He unpacks and heads to the bathroom. In between knocking over the toothbrush holder and banging his knees on the bath, he decides that they need a bigger place.

He also thinks about what he will say to Marcia. Micah's squeal breaks his concentration, and she hugs him as hard as she can and smothers the side of his face with kisses.

She chats nineteen to the dozen – school things, play things, music things, clothes things. Then she says, "and Marcia took me to this huge museum full of things and we ate ice cream in the biggest park I have ever seen and then we went to the pictures. She is so nice daddy."

He smiles back. "So, you don't need my presents since you so busy getting all cultured on me."

She looks shocked and then she laughs. "Daddy, you are so silly, of course I want my presents."

They go to his room and he hands her a bag stuffed with clothes, books and sticks of sweet rock. More hugs and kisses and a mini fashion show, and then she runs downstairs to show her granny all her treasures.

Her mess – bags, wrapping paper and her school bag – make his room even smaller.

He changes his clothes, and after breakfast he heads out the door. In his pocket is an envelope.

WHO JAH BLESS,
NO MAN CURSE

Dante waits outside of Marcia's office block and studies the people walking in and out. They move quickly and look joyless. He is not sure what time she finishes work, or if she was even at work today. After an hour a woman approaches him. She smiles and says his name.

He stands straight and looks right at her. "Yes."

"Marcia's gonna be another ten minutes or so. Do you want to wait in reception?"

He instinctively looks at the office block and the hundreds of windows, then nods and follows the lady across the road. The reception area is bright, and the walls are covered in pictures of women wearing too much make up, with strange hairstyles, and they are mainly white. He picks up a magazine and flicks through the pages, but nothing catches his attention. He is saved by Marcia's voice as she enters the reception area.

He stands up, and is suddenly unsure of what he should do – kiss her, or shake her hand? So he nods at her and she nods back. They walk out of the reception area side by side, without a word passing between them until they are safely on the sidewalk.

"You good?" asks Dante.

"Yes." Her voice is clear, and not as sad as the last time they spoke.

"You want to go somewhere to talk?"

"Ok."

Dante touches the envelope in his pocket as they continue walking. She touches his arm as they reach a small bar.

They sit down at a small table just beside the front door. Marcia smiles with the waitress and ask for a menu.

"You come here a lot?"

"After work sometimes."

He studies the menu; the food sounds small and foreign.

He looks up and finds Marcia studying him.

"What's wrong?"

He does not answer straight away. He tries to smile, but instead, he sighs.

"You hungry?"

"Not really, you?"

"Not sure, this food don't look like anything I want to eat."

Marcia laughs, and Dante realises that he misses this sound. He places his hand on hers and she smiles.

They start talking about their days – her writing, and his tour and offers of more writing gigs. They dance a sweet duet without really facing up to the one issue.

Marcia eventually orders drinks and some crackers and pâté. Dante tries some, and it tastes like the stuff his mum used to buy at the supermarket in small glass jars. He grimaces and sticks to his glass of warm beer.

They do not speak anymore until after he pays the bill. He wants to stay in her presence.

"You want to go to the pictures?"

"Now?"

"Why not, you got anything planned?"

"No, ok."

"What do you fancy seeing?"

"You choose."

They stand in front of the pictures.

Dante pays for two tickets to a new Peter Sellers comedy. He then buys two popcorn and two soft drinks.

They sit in the darkness holding hands, and for 90 minutes they laugh and Marcia lays her head on his shoulder and he leans towards her.

Dante goes over the picture, scene by scene, and Marcia laughs. This easiness between them continues all the way until they reach her bedsit.

"It was good being with you Marcia... Look, I got to take Micah to school in the morning, so best I chip home."

Marcia nods and steps forward. She kisses him and he holds her. He likes the way she smells. He holds her a little longer.

"I best chip. Here, read this and tell me what you think."

He hands her the envelope and kisses her one more time.

He sleeps well that night, and when he comes home from taking Micah to school he finds Marcia in the kitchen with his mum.

"Hi."

"Hi."

His mum gets up, muttering something about having to go to the post office, shops and market.

Dante and Marcia hug and kiss.

"I read it all night. Dante, your writing is so sure and real. I cried, I laughed. When did you write this?"

"The nights after we went to the clinic." The word abortion is still too hard a word to say.

She nods.

"Are there more words like this?"

He nods and leads her to his room. He pulls out a box from the bottom of his wardrobe, and it is full of exercise books. Marcia sits on the floor and reads through the daylight hours, while Dante sits downstairs watching the television.

Micah and his mother return, filling the house with their voices and energy. The smell of cooking and sound of footsteps up and down the stairs do not move him. He is listening for Marcia, and the longer she stays upstairs the more afraid he feels.

His mum calls them all to the kitchen for dinner and Marcia emerges, eyes bright and wet. Yet, she is smiling. His mum and Micah do not look surprised to see her as they sit down to eat. Micah begins the conversation and it ebbs and flows with a rhythm as familiar as Dante's own breathing...

GLOSSARY

Beanie – Groupie.

Black maria – Police van for transporting prisoners.

Blues party/dance – Private party usually held in a house, empty flat or basement and requiring payment on entry. Their heyday was in the 1970s and 1980s in Britain's Black communities.

Brew (see Special Brew).

Lovers rock – A style of reggae music noted for its romantic sound and content.

Roach, Colin – 21-year-old Black British man who died from a gunshot wound inside the entrance of Stoke Newington police station in east London on 12 January 1983. Amid allegations of a police cover-up, the case became a cause célèbre for civil rights campaigners and Black community groups in the United Kingdom.

Rizla – Popular brand of cigarette rolling papers.

Rodigan, David – English radio DJ renowned for playing reggae and dancehall music on London-based radio stations since the late 1970s.

Special Brew – Brand of super-strength lager.

SUS / SUS law – Informal name for a 'stop and search' law that was used by the police. It was used to particularly target Black and ethnic minority people. The acronym is a contraction of 'suspected person'.